A KISS OF WINTER

A SECOND CHANCE CHRISTMAS ROMANCE - DREAMS FULFILLED BOOK 3

SCARLETT KING

CONTENTS

Sign Up to Receive Free Books	v
Synopsis	vii

1. Andi	1
2. David	8
3. Andi	14
4. David	22
5. Andi	29
6. David	38
7. Andi	45
8. David	53
9. Andi	69
10. David	78

Sign Up to Receive Free Books	81
Preview of His Hidden Love	83
Chapter One - Wicked Game	87
Chapter Two - I'll Be Seeing You	93
Chapter Three - Let's Get Lost	103
Chapter Four - Faded	109
Chapter Five - Pretty	113
Chapter Six - Here with Me	115
Chapter Seven - Rid of Me	121
Chapter Eight - Million Dollar Man	129
Chapter Nine - Every Breath You Take	135
Chapter Ten - Perfectly Lonely	143
Chapter Eleven - Angel	153
Chapter Twelve - Love is a Losing Game	159
Other Books By This Author	169

Made in "The United States" by:

Alizeh Valentine

© Copyright 2020 – Alizeh Valentine

ISBN: 978-1-64808-120-0

ALL RIGHTS RESERVED. No part of this publication may be reproduced or transmitted in any form whatsoever, electronic, or mechanical, including photocopying, recording, or by any informational storage or retrieval system without express written, dated and signed permission from the author

❦ Created with Vellum

SIGN UP TO RECEIVE FREE BOOKS

Sign Up to Receive Free E-Books and Audiobook Codes.

Would you like to read **The Unexpected Nanny, Dirty Little Virgin** and **other romance books** for **free**?

You can sign up to receive these free e-books and audiobooks by typing this link into your browser:

https://www.steamyromance.info/free-books-and-audiobooks-hot-and-steamy/

Or this one:

https://www.steamyromance.info/the-unexpected-nanny-free/

SYNOPSIS

Andi Carter and David Delgado are best friends and partners in a ghost hunting organization in Upstate New York. They also used to be married—but they don't like to talk about that. It was a mistake, they were too young...and there were some issues in their sex life. Once again—they don't talk about it. Of course, now they're back in the land of unresolved sexual tension, Mulder and Scullying their way through cases—except that he's the skeptic.

They hear about a bizarre case in picturesque Phoenicia, and head out to a bed and breakfast to investigate for themselves. Once there, the romantic setting creates hilarious levels of awkwardness as their memory of their comically terrible first try intrudes on any hope for a second chance. They try to focus on the investigation, but can't seem to sort out where the mistletoe came from or how it manages to keep being replaced.

When a few of the locals start flirting with them, unexpected jealousy and rekindling of desire force the pair to work on solving their own romantic issues. Their rekindled passions end up reminding them of the love they share, and give them a second chance now that they are mature enough to form a committed relationship. In that way their hunt is a success, even if the mistletoe incident remains a mystery forever.

∼

Andi

David and I don't talk about our short-lived marriage. It gets in the way of our friendship and our partnership. We're supposed to be trying to explain the inexplicable—of the paranormal variety, not the romantic—and bickering about our ill-fated romance isn't the way to do it.

We were so young back then, and though he was never able to satisfy me when we were both inexperienced and didn't have a clue, being cooped up with him in this romantic little town has me noticing how much David has changed—and has me wondering just how much he's truly learned in the years since we broke up.

With mistletoe hanging everywhere in this town, there's no doubt that love is in the air. But can that love be ours, or did we already waste our one chance? 'Tis the season for many things, but are we brave enough to let it be the season of second chances?

∼

David

Once upon a time I was a complete idiot—too damn young

and inexperienced and cocky to boot. And because of that, I messed up my chances with the woman I've always loved.

Unrequited love is never easy, but it's a whole hell of a lot harder when it includes a successful business and a lifelong friendship. Even years after I blew my chance, I just can't let go of the feeling that Andi is the only one for me.

I never want to see Andi hurt again, so when she comes down with a mysterious winter-related illness, all my protective instincts come creeping in. I've already lost this woman once, and I'll be damned if it happens again.

Now I just need to make her see that we're worth a second chance—and if I need to let a little Christmas magic run its course to make that happen...well then, who am I to say that miracles don't exist?

1
ANDI

"**G**ood morning, sunshine!"

David strolls in through the connecting door between our suites and pulls the curtains aside on all the windows, sending thin winter sunlight trickling into the room. He's got that shit-eating grin on his handsome face that used to annoy me back when we were married.

I lob my pillow at him, eyes bleary, but my aim is still perfect after five years. It bounces off his chest, and he looks down, then snorts and scoops it up. I roll over and bury my face in my remaining pillow. "Go away! It's freezing and before nine."

"Yes, and this is the Catskills. People start their days at dawn here—we're missing chances for interviews. Besides, it was your idea for us to spend our Christmas up here." The slight edge to his voice reminds me of how hard it had been to sell him on this investigation when I first learned of the events transpiring in this town.

Our partnership as paranormal investigators—just like our friendship—survived our disastrous six-month marriage with little more than some awkwardness and regret. But here I've had to live with him again for over a week and a half, and it's reminding me of why we broke up. "Yes, I know. Just give me... half an hour."

I have also always hated that he's a morning person.

"Nuh-uh. You decided to spend half the night driving over to the county hospital to chase down those frostbite cases, and you straight up told me that you didn't want us knocked off schedule because of it." He comes over and crouches down beside the bed, so his face is level with mine. "So get your cute ass up. We have a mystery to solve."

He was right. And it wasn't just any mystery, either. It was the paranormal event of a lifetime—a genuine Christmas miracle that started almost two weeks ago with thousands of witnesses. It was an event so enormous that even news and social media have noticed and have been rationalizing and celebrating it instead of denying it outright.

Within a week of the first sighting on December 23rd, Phoenicia, New York, had already gained the nickname Mistletoe Village, becoming a destination for romantic-minded snow bunnies from all over the East Coast—and beyond. The bed and breakfasts have filled up, people are renting out spare rooms in their houses for some extra cash, and over a hundred couples have gotten engaged here so far. Tourists, reporters, bloggers, and curiosity seekers are mingling with the local population, filling up the restaurants, cafes, and bars as the early January chill drives them inside.

I can hear the rustle and chatter of the crowd down on the street even through my double-glazed window. *Dammit, he's right.*

I sigh into my bedding and roll over to look at David. He's cute, both in personality and looks, and I really like the guy. But I also find him really annoying at times, which is part of why the whole marriage thing never worked out.

We're still best friends though, and I wouldn't be able to run

Astraea Paranormal without him. He's the tech half to my lore half. While I'm doing interviews, conducting research, and recording EVPs, he's checking for magnetic fields, seeking rational explanations, and making sure that whatever we come up with can't be easily debunked. He also handles the technical and scheduling details, making sure we can get where we need to be and do what we need to do—and do it on time.

And that's why I'm waking up on January the third in a bed and breakfast in the Catskills with my ex-husband in my face.

"Dammit, Dave," I grumble, but I know he's right.

David Delgado, tech genius and occasional jackass who was born with a silver spoon in his mouth, flops into a bedside chair as I drag myself out of bed. He's the classic tall, dark, and handsome type with thick, coffee-colored hair, big brown eyes, and an easy smile. To top it off, I know he's got an amazing body under that turtleneck and jeans—but I don't let myself think about that any more.

When he was younger, he was almost cherubic looking. But he was also a bit of an immature pain in the butt back then, so... it was a trade-off.

And that brings us to Reason Number Two that we should never have married: we were too damn young to know what we were doing—in and out of bed. It would have helped if David had taken instruction better, but I have my own faults, too.

I rub my eyes, blinking several times. "Unh. Okay. My notes from last night's interviews are on the laptop. Take a look at them while I clean up." I push myself out of bed as he gets up to go for my laptop case.

As I walk past him, I hear his breath catch. Still half asleep, I haven't pulled my sleeping shirt down to cover where it's ridden up my thighs in back. I grumble and tug the hem down over my ass, remembering how I used to love turning him on by accident like that.

"Y-yeah. Okay," he replies like a startled kid. I can't help but smile a little. Okay, well, maybe I still like it some.

My marriage to David was the biggest and most regrettable mistake I've made in my life. We were too young—in our early twenties—and though David is sweet and would never hurt me, he was even more in over his head than I was. He was too immature and irritating to live with, and it sometimes felt like I was helping to raise my younger brother all over again.

As I scrub off in the shower with the door open, I hear him clicking away on my laptop. "I'm really starting to think someone is messing with our investigation," I hear him sigh.

"That Jack Whitman guy?" I think about Whitman as I lather up my hair. He's a local—and a world-class skier, snow sculptor, and billionaire playboy with an eccentric father. Mischievous, creative and—I'm starting to suspect—probably the reason why we're here.

He also happens to be ridiculously sexy in that slim, toned, sleek way that is almost androgynous. With his pale white skin, black hair, his father's brilliant blue eyes, and one of those smiles that light up the street, it's a real shame that he's even less mature than David.

"Whitman and whoever else is conspiring with him to do this. There is absolutely no way that mistletoe could just appear hanging just about everywhere in the entire town, with new sprigs somehow popping up every night, without an awful lot of help." I hear more typing.

"You're presuming that nothing paranormal is going on." I have soap in my eyes. "Crap." I bend into the spray to rinse it out and then rinse out my hair, enjoying the hot water on my skin. New York winters leave a chill that's hard to get out of your bones, but a shower or a soak does the trick, even if only for a short while.

"It's my job to presume that nothing paranormal is going

on." He taps a few keys. "Did you actually find out anything from the nurses?"

"They wouldn't let me record, but I got some follow-ups. The Marysville Hospital serves this entire area, and until they get an accident or a bad bug going around, they're usually pretty quiet." I turn the water off and stand in the steam, rubbing conditioner into my thick auburn hair.

"So the frostbite thing stood out?"

"Not for that in particular. They get frostbite cases every year, and there was just a big storm. But no. I was pretty much able to verify that it was the two troublemakers we've been tracking, though." I massage the conditioner through my hair, keeping half an eye on the open door through the steamed-up shower glass. I've caught David peeking before.

"How did you manage that? Bribery?" He sounds intrigued.

"Not really. They didn't violate anyone's privacy by actually naming names. But their description of 'that redhead diva bitch who claimed she got frostbite on her nose out of nowhere and then exploded when the surgeon said amputation might be necessary,' sounds a lot like Andrea Case. And 'that drunk biker who was in here twice in three days for frostbite and for getting maced by the other patient,' sounds an awful lot like Daniel Gates."

"That's a good point." More typing. "Oh, great...you finished the write-up of your interview with them last night?"

"Yeah, I wanted to get it down in writing while it was fresh." I hate interviews where they won't let me record.

"This is eight pages. No wonder you're worn out. What time did you finally get to sleep?" Now he sounds worried, which makes me feel a bit guilty.

I shake it off after a moment. "I wasn't looking at the clock."

"Tch. You work too hard." I hear one of the interviews start to play: the one with Jack.

"*All right, so,*" I hear my own voice, which sounds tinny and strange in recordings. I try to ignore that as I listen. "*Please state your name, age, hometown, and occupation for the record.*"

Jack's laughing voice takes over. "*My name's Jack Frost, as I told you before. I'm ageless, I live at the North Pole with my father Saint Nicholas, and my job is bringing the fall colors and the winter frosts.*"

A long, awkward pause. "*I understand that you're in character for the kids and all, but—*"

"*Oh, is that what I'm doing?*" His tone teases me.

"Does this guy have to troll us each and every time that we get him on camera?" Delgado grumbles. "Hurry up. I want to go over this stuff with you before we grab some breakfast."

"I'm not entirely sure that he is trolling us," I say thoughtfully as I rinse out my hair. "He does have a weird sense of humor, but so does his dad, and these are the guys who made sure the local food bank had a surplus right before the holiday."

"Do you think he and his dad are delusional?" he asks seriously, stopping the video.

"I don't know. But if they are, it's the most benign delusion ever. As far as I can tell, pretty much everyone up here loves them, even if nobody past the age of five believes that they're anything but ordinary people." I finish the shower and close the door most of the way so that I can towel off and dress.

"Okay, yeah. I admit his dad is pretty cool. But I don't trust this guy." He hesitates then says slowly, "He's wasting our time. And he keeps hitting on you."

I stop short in the middle of pulling on my long underwear, hearing a faint alarm bell go off in the back of my head. He's not wrong; Jack is a flirt.

That's not the problem. The problem is that after all this time, David should know better than to be jealous. And yet I'm hearing that tone in his voice.

It takes everything I have to keep the awkward laugh out of

my own voice as I finish dressing. "He hits on every woman who's over the age of eighteen and isn't wearing a ring. What's your point?"

Another pause. "Oh." He sounds a little calmer suddenly, and I roll my eyes. "Well, he just annoys me."

"Yeah, well, he's a bit immature, and immaturity is annoying." So is jealousy, especially when it's coming from a guy who had his chance and blew it. "Give me a minute, and let's go over the new stuff before breakfast."

I have to get things back on track. If David is starting to think of me as his again—if he's getting jealous—then we have a problem. We're on the brink of proving the paranormal origin of an ongoing town-wide phenomenon. I don't have time for David's romantic regrets.

Or my own.

2

DAVID

"So according to the nurses, the biker was recovering from hypothermia and mild frostbite when he was picked up by state police." I lean toward the laptop screen with Andi beside me, trying to ignore how nice her freshly-washed hair smells. I really don't have time for inconvenient boners.

The biggest mistake I have ever made in my life, contrary to the beliefs of my family, wasn't my getting into paranormal investigation when I'm not even a believer myself. And it also wasn't the time I blew a hundred thousand dollars of Dad's money in Monaco when I was twenty. It wasn't even when I let a former partner take one of my inventions as his severance—a patent that turned out to be worth millions.

It was, quite simply, letting the woman of my dreams slip through my fingers.

Andromeda "Andi" Carter really is the whole package. Smart, ambitious, imaginative, hot, pretty, and sweet. At sixteen, I wanted to get into her pants so badly that I couldn't breathe, but of course, she put me off. At twenty, I finally did get into her pants—and I loved every minute of it. Not that there were ever too many minutes to savor at one time.

But Andi, well, she never seemed to enjoy it as much as I did. Which always frustrated me. At the time, I thought there was something wrong with her when she didn't like exactly what I liked in bed, when I liked it. But I was the typical selfish twenty-year-old guy back then with my brain mostly located at the end of my dick.

I know better now, but it's too late. Our problems in bed were just one of many other issues that drove us apart. Eight months after I made love to her for the first time, she packed her bags and left.

We patched things up enough to keep Astraea together as well as our friendship. But I still wonder to this day what would have happened if we'd waited until we both had grown up more. Would it have lasted? Would it last if we tried again now?

"How did you find out that Andrea Case was the one who maced him?" I ask Andi as I look up from her notes.

"They got into a fistfight in the waiting room." She winces as she speaks, and I stifle an outburst of laughter.

"Oh man, this town." I rub my face and look back at her notes. "Well, that does it for the written stuff. Let's have a look at the rest of yesterday's interviews and then grab some breakfast."

"Sounds good to me. I'm starving." She's sitting next to me brushing her hair out. The rich smell of her hair mixes with the fruity shampoo and tickles my nostrils. As much as I love the smell of her, I have to keep reminding myself that she's not mine.

Some days, I'm fine with that. Others, it's like a fucking Greek tragedy that I simply can't escape, leaving me wondering why I wasn't prescient enough to see the writing on the wall back then. Right now, being so close to Andi makes me want to slip an arm around her and beg her to take me back.

Ugh, too bad it's too early for a drink.

"So what's our amended timeline?" she asks as she pulls up a few interviews.

I bring the timeline file up on my smartphone. "December 23rd at dawn, the mistletoe appears. Nobody sees who put it up or who keeps replacing it when it's taken down. Mistletoe is everywhere including private houses and the interior of the church. The night of the 25th, a snowstorm hits, damaging outdoor decorations and blacking out half the town. When we dig out the next morning, the mistletoe had stayed up. Either it resisted wind that ripped branches off trees in a few places, or somehow someone put it all back up after the storm without being seen or leaving tracks in the snow."

It sounds absolutely ridiculous to me, except that I saw that last part with my own eyes. The stuff simply doesn't stay down for long. The pastor, who keeps clearing his grounds of mistletoe since he doesn't want people sucking face in the church graveyard, complained about it to me. He also mentioned, once again, that when it's replaced, no footprints are left in the snow.

That one detail—that one inexplicable thing—is what's kept me here even though this could be one of our most boring investigations yet. All we do most of the day is push through crowds and plod around chasing down rumors about what's happening. The mistletoe keeps reappearing over new snow with no footprints.

How bizarre is that?

"Is there any chance that the whole town is in on it? Maybe it's just a stunt to create this tourism boom?" I ask slowly and thoughtfully. "Or maybe as a little Christmas magic for the kids?"

She shakes her head after a brief, thoughtful silence. "No. It's created too much disruption. And because of how people react to it: everyone we interviewed seems baffled. If everyone was in on it, then a lot of the townspeople would have to be amazing amateur actors."

I sit back, tapping my lips with my finger. The motive is plausible, but the execution...

She's right. It would be impossible or nearly so. One of the Whitmans or someone else must have hired a small team of people who have been sneaking around. Or...something. I'm not crediting anything supernatural. Not yet.

"Okay, we already have the transcripts of Jack's comments." She leans forward slightly as she brings his interview recording back up. It's stopped in the middle, frozen on a single frame of his irritatingly handsome face.

God, I hate this guy. Not just because he flirts with Andi in front of me, not just because he doesn't really seem to do anything useful with his time and wealth, but because Andi seems...interested. And I'm not handling that well.

Even though I've taken some casual lovers over the years, there's never been anyone else for me besides Andi. I think it might be the same for her—in fact, I don't think she's dated since she packed her bags and left our home. Maybe I should feel bad about that. I kind of worry that some of my behavior left her jaded about relationships.

Yeah. It was that big of a screw-up. I'm not proud of it.

There's part of me that gets stupid romantic sometimes and thinks that maybe Andi's never dated anyone else because she's been waiting for me to grow up. That maybe she'll give me another shot now that she knows I've got my shit together.

But that's probably stupid. I had my shot. I shouldn't be jealous if she decides to move on.

Except I really, really am jealous. I know it's a problem. I hope that she doesn't notice...but I know it's a slim hope. Andi notices everything.

Sitting side by side, we start playing through the interview with the sound on low, watching Jack Whitman's expressions and gestures. I never trust a guy that smiles that much, and I hope that Andi doesn't either. Fortunately, she's smart, and she doesn't put up with bad treatment.

She'll catch on to his bullshit soon enough and brush him off. Not that it's any of my business. After all, she's not mine anymore. *But I still give a shit about her, and this guy is bad news. I can feel it.*

"Hold on a second," she says, pausing the tape. "That shop window right there that he's leaning next to." She points to the window in question.

"That's the candy store. What am I looking at?"

"By his face." She taps the screen, and I peer at the image. Jack has leaned over against the storefront window and is blowing on it softly, the mist of his breath making a fern pattern of frost on the glass.

"Weird," she mumbles.

"What's weird? It's freezing, and he breathed on the glass. Of course it fogged up and then frosted over." I stare at the frost pattern, wondering just what it is that has captivated her. "I used to see them on the old shed at my grandmother's farmhouse every winter when I was a kid."

"It's not the frost itself. It's the form it's taking. Windows used to get that fern frond pattern on them in winter back in the days of single glazing, like on your grandmother's shed. But it shouldn't happen on a sheet of shop glass."

I'm not following. Maybe this is an upstate thing—she's the one who grew up around here. If anyone would know, it's her. "Why?"

"Almost all of the home and shop windows around here are double and triple glazed. They're a lot more insulated, so you don't get the level of heat loss that causes those patterns on the glass." She's toying with the end of her braid, looking thoughtful.

"Are you sure? Some of the buildings around here are really old—they could have the original glass." I try not to stare at her too obviously, but this is one of countless cute little gestures of hers that make me want to hug her—and drag her off to bed to show her what I've learned. I struggle to shift my focus back to the conversation.

She nods once. "Only one way to find out. I want to get a look at that shop window as soon as we have some food in us."

"Fair enough. Let's just...not do so much legwork outside today, all right? It's twelve degrees out."

She gives me a lopsided smile. "You were the one who was so eager to get going a half hour ago when you were dragging me out of bed. Now come on, we can warm up with cocoa breaks every now and again while we're out."

"As long as the cocoa is spiked." A man has to put his foot down sometime, and if I have to endure another day of pounding the streets of this tiny town in freezing weather, I'm not doing it totally sober.

"The warmth you get from booze is fake. You know that." She frowns at me worriedly, and I snort.

I shrug. "'Tis the fucking season." I shut down the laptop and get up to bundle into my outerwear.

Her frown dissolves and a twinkle of humor enters her eyes. "All right, fair enough."

3
ANDI

We're getting closer to the truth. I can feel it. The idea sings in my head as David and I load our plates at the breakfast buffet and take seats across from each other at a small table. "I'm pretty sure we're headed for a breakthrough," I say confidently as we settle in.

He looks up at me with dull sarcasm in his eyes that just screams, *'Are you kidding?'*

"Food, coffee," he mumbles around his first forkful of eggs. "No talk."

It stops me short, and I let out a little laugh as he scoops more of his scrambled eggs into his mouth. I take a bite of my waffles, and my own appetite wakes up.

We eat in silence for a while. It's easy and relaxed, not awkward like it was when I first broke up with him. On those mornings, sitting across from each other at my breakfast table in the Boston Tudor I've since sold, the silence between us was packed full of tension.

Now, we're just stuffing our faces with good country fare and a whole lot of coffee. Outside the window, snow is drifting down again. People crowd down the packed streets as if it were midsummer, bundled against the cold, trying to ignore the snow blowing into their faces.

Phoenicia sure is pretty. It's one of those little towns that you whip past on the highway, with its own sign and exit, but with hills and tall trees concealing large parts of the town. It's thriving compared to a lot of these isolated highway-side towns, mostly because it caters to tourists with businesses like the old-timey theater and river rafting.

But it's normally not thriving like this. The breakfast room is crowded. Parking spots are filled everywhere that I can see. And foot traffic is constantly being held up by the ever-present mistletoe with some couples stopping every couple of minutes to participate in the novelty.

It's pretty cute to watch—people stealing kisses in the cold. But it makes me a little sad, too. I see the way David looks at me when he thinks I don't notice, and it makes me wistful. I have always wondered what it would be like if I gave him a second chance. It just never seemed...smart. So I never tried it.

But times like this, watching the little scenes of romance and the awkwardness of young love on the snowy street, I'm reminded too much of my cold and lonely bed. Sometimes I miss him, though I tell myself I just miss having someone at my side who cares about me. No matter how frustrated David made me, at least I always knew that he gave a damn. And I know that he always will—even if he sometimes has no idea at all how to express it.

"You know," he says finally, once he's caffeinated enough that his eyes aren't dull, "there's one thing I haven't asked you. What exactly is the theory we're working from in this case?"

"Sorry, what?" I ask distractedly. I just noticed Jack outside. He's idly gliding along in his boots down a strip of ice that has formed after repeated passes by the plows. His hands are tucked behind his back, his midnight blue coat and dark hair flap in the breeze, and he's smiling with mischievous amusement.

Of course he grabs my attention easily. Jack has…glamour. That's the only way I can describe it. I have been in the presence of millionaires, scientific geniuses, industry giants, and movie stars…but Jack manages to outshine them all—without seeming to make much of an effort.

Who is he really? I wonder, and then catch myself and look back at David.

"Are we here because there's simply another kind of unknown phenomenon going on? If that's the case, what are we saying that phenomenon is? We have to go beyond a 'Christmas miracle' and get at some specifics." He stabs at one of his sausages as I tear my eyes away from the gorgeous man gliding past…yet again.

His question catches me by surprise. I'm not sure I've ever given him a working theory beyond telling him, *"This is obviously supernatural. Let's see what we can catch on tape."* On the other hand, we've never spent over a week in the cold, away from our families on the holidays, to chase what could be our first real proof of the supernatural. Nor has it ever been this big, with this many witnesses.

"Give me a moment," I mutter over the rim of my coffee mug. "This is a little hard to put into words."

"It always is," he grumbles, and I feel a stab of worry. He sees my face and just offers a tight smile. "Sorry. I'm just sick of the snow. Can't we just go ghost hunting in New Orleans for a few months?"

"That's actually damn tempting," I admit as the tension breaks, and he lets out a little laugh. "No, seriously. You're right. We're probably going to end up presenting on this at the conventions, so I had better have my thoughts organized."

He nods slowly and waits for me, staring broodingly out the

window. I catch the exact moment that he notices Jack: his expression darkens, his eyes narrow slightly. I swallow and look down at the tabletop, trying to gather my thoughts.

In all the years we've been doing this—meticulously cataloging supernatural events and testing their validity, publishing books, giving talks at conventions, and interviews for blogs and podcasts—there's never been one single big discovery like this. No 'Aha!' moment where we absolutely knew we had proof that people would have to believe. Plenty of hopeful moments—and a lot of letdowns—but we've never found our Holy Grail.

We've come close: the haunted house in North Carolina with the constant scrambling sounds in its walls but no signs of infestation; the San Francisco vampire that really did have what looked to be a photo of himself from 1863—even if David swears to this day that the guy in the picture was just a doppelganger.

We've come back from our investigations with proof that impresses those in our field, and we've managed to make a name for ourselves among American parapsychologists. The problem is that we can never convince *everyone* to let go of their preconceived beliefs and take in new information. No matter how convincing our evidence, people always want to run it through their cultural, religious, and personal filters—just like David does.

And that's what makes our job so challenging. It's also helped us learn how to cover all our tracks and be meticulous about our research and theories.

"The only working theory that I have so far is that whoever is responsible for this, their motives would be the same regardless of whether or not they are using some kind of supernatural ability to pull this off. It's a boost to the town—its economy, its reputation, its celebration of the holiday..." I'm rambling, I realize. I go quiet, cheeks heating up a little.

He sits forward. "Okay, that part I can get behind. Go on."

"Our prime suspects are Jack and his father, Dr. Whitman. Do we even know if their familial connection has ever been confirmed?" A lot of the local 'information' on people seems to be based on assumptions and rumors.

I'm used to the New York rumor mill; it churns 24/7 in small towns and big cities. It is even worse on the Internet: from whispers in boardrooms to breathless social media posts by tween girls, it runs an endless stream of what-ifs, fluff, filler, and bullshit—and sometimes, the occasional gem. Like the collection of local folklore surrounding the Whitmans.

"Very little about Dr. Whitman is confirmed, except for his history of propping up the town every winter with donations, benefits, and parties. As for Jack, he has a confirmed career as a hotshot local skier and playboy with a whole lot of awards and prizes." He's reading from the file on his phone.

That makes me feel better about spending so much time getting everything updated last night. I wasn't sleeping anyway, but it is still nice to know that I spent my bout of insomnia being productive. "Nobody's entirely sure what kind of doctor Whitman is, though. Some say he has a PhD in folklore, some says he's a pediatrician, some say he's a child psychologist. There's a whole list. Scroll down two pages," I tell him.

"Oh wait." He flicks his finger over his phone screen and pauses to swallow down more coffee.

I'm still working on my eggs. I've been eating more slowly than usual, my attention all over the place, what with the investigation, the holiday, David, Jack, the sex dreams I've been having about both of them since we got here…

I cover my face with my hands, blushing furiously. I've been trying not to think about those, especially in David's presence.

It's true, though. It's the reason I couldn't sleep last night. Better that I lose sleep than wake up feeling that way again—

heated but unsatisfied, but mostly frustrated as hell from the images my mind teases me with.

But I can't help it. My head keeps filling up with images and sensations that have never happened, but that I wish would. If only things were different.

In one dream, I'm wrestling with Jack on an honest to God pile of furs over who gets to be on top. He's laughing playfully and letting me win…sometimes. There's snow falling outside the odd little cottage, and the icy draft whistling past the window panes bites any bit of my skin not covered by the furs—or him—but the heat inside of me seems to burn it away.

And then there are the dreams about David. David making me feel pleasure for hours on end, instead of turning me on and then leaving me lying there cold, confused, and frustrated.

Though my dream self doesn't seem to have any issues finding release, my real self isn't so lucky. I don't know how it feels to climax, and no matter how hot my dreams are, my body just won't go that far on images alone. I keep waking up shaking and sweaty—aching with unfulfilled need.

I don't like dwelling on David's failings as a husband, because if I do I end up getting this stabbing headache in my temples that I can't get rid of for hours. And then I can't handle being around David for a while.

I remind myself of a few things as I wait for David to finish skimming the file. It helps keep my old frustrations at bay.

First, after our breakup and after spending a few years speaking to other women about their own failed romances, I learned that David was pretty typical of early twenties guys—both in bed and out. I could have forgiven his flakiness, his goofiness, and even the sexual inexperience if he had been willing to admit to it, to listen, and to learn. But he was convinced he knew everything already, and I quickly got too frustrated to deal with that.

Turns out, most young guys seem to think they know everything about sex—or are at least too proud to admit that they don't.

If only I had known, I might have been more patient and kept trying. Or I would have at least found another way to approach the subject.

In my dreams, I get a taste of what might have happened if I had. And it's heartbreaking.

I've never had an orgasm in my life. For a while after our relationship ended, David's voice stayed in my head, blaming me for being 'uptight.' It lingered, even though I had fought back at the time, demanding to know what a guy with an 'I'm going in dry' T-shirt could possibly know about satisfying women.

In the end, we both lost. I learned the hard way not to get too serious too fast, especially when you're just starting out. Knowing someone as a friend and knowing them as a lover and potential husband, it turns out, are two very, very different things.

David learned the hard way that if you can't please your woman, and you don't want to learn, then you don't get to blame her for that. You don't call her frigid, you don't ask what's wrong with her, and you don't otherwise add insult to injury by being a shitty lover and then calling her one.

And if you do, then you'd better get ready for her to unload six months of sexual frustration, humiliation, and heartbreak at you in one five-minute verbal barrage, and then watch her turn around and start packing her things.

I shake myself out of my reverie to see that David is chuckling obliviously, probably over some of the Whitman folklore I gathered while he was interviewing some of the store owners. I surreptitiously wipe my eyes, face turned toward the window.

Jack is out there, chatting and laughing a little with a big biker guy that I peg after a second as Daniel Gates's brother, Aaron.

Aaron seems to be in an awfully good mood for a guy whose brother went straight from the hospital to jail recently. Curiosity distracts me enough that some of my sadness lifts. My failure to launch with David is in the past, after all. I've already decided not to let it ruin the present.

How I wish I could have had just one single night with him that was even half as good as my dreams.

4

DAVID

I'm trying to pretend I don't notice, but something's going on with Andi. I know she didn't sleep much, but even factoring that in, she seems...distracted. Unhappy.

I'm trying not to bring it up, because that's an emotional minefield I can't risk crossing. It's possible that she's just as sick of Phoenicia as I am. Or maybe she's worn out from the cold, the holiday season, and all the legwork we've been doing.

Or maybe being around me is making her unhappy.

I try to dismiss that last idea as stupid and pointless, but the truth is, I just don't know. The holidays are a tough time for a lot of singles. They are for me. Andi is more romantic than I am, and I'm a little worried that it affects her more.

I'll ask her what's up in private later, if she doesn't seem to be getting better. I know it's none of my business—at least not beyond the concern of a friend, anyway. I don't want to make her feel smothered.

It's been rough, these years of pretending I'm not still in love with her. It's roughest when she's hurting. I see her in pain, just within hugging range, but I know that if I touch her like that then I'm at risk for a bad case of boner-brain and all the awkwardness that comes with it. Not to mention that it would probably just add to her discomfort.

Being a gentleman about this is tough sometimes. But I'd rather have her in my life as a friend and business partner than not at all. And I don't want to make her unhappy again. Landing such an awesome woman and then finding out that I'd driven her away by making her miserable—without even realizing I was doing it—was the worst wake-up call of my life.

It's so easy to rationalize every annoying, destructive habit you have when you're only focused on yourself. But when you're living with another person, and they have to deal with all those flaws—or worst case, get hurt and irritated by them—being oblivious like that has a high cost. Most kids in their early twenties don't have everything figured out right away, and clearly Andi and I didn't, either.

The problem was my assumption that I did, in fact, know everything there was to know about love, sex, and relationships, and her assumption that I should. At twenty-two, I was still figuring out tax forms and how much alcohol I could drink safely without waking up in the hospital. She has admitted since that her expectations were too high—but some of them really, really weren't.

I keep pretending to read the report I already read this morning, to give her a minute. I hope that she's not staring out the window just so she can catch a glimpse of Jack. I know he's out there, chatting with the local bouncer.

I go back to the file on my phone. "I like this one the best. The one about Dr. Whitman being a Navy medic who is covered with tattoos under his shirt, one for each person he's killed."

She looks back at me, and her smile flickers to life again. "Yeah, and supposedly he's so nice now because he's trying to repent for all he's done. Unfortunately, I think we can write that one off as a colorful fiction." But then she glances back out the window. "The question is, how do we verify which, if any, of these stories about Whitman are true?"

"We're gonna have to finally pin him down for an interview. I don't care if we have to do it in the middle of a damn snowstorm—he's not putting us off again. He's our prime suspect. If we can prove he's behind the mistletoe, then it will all boil down to what method he used. Mundane, or...not so mundane."

Though I really suspect we'll just find out he hired a bunch of agile kids to sneak around putting up mistletoe for fun and for getting his town some good press.

"I guess I was worried that when you were asking me what our working theory was, that it would come out a lot more far-fetched than 'a local philanthropist is probably behind this, but we're not certain if he used magic or not.' At least with this we have something to work with still." Now her smile comes alongside an self-conscious laugh.

"Oh, you mean like: 'A local philanthropist is actually Santa Claus'? Yeah, that is far-fetched." I can't keep the teasing note out of my voice, and she laughs in embarrassment.

"I wasn't gonna say it like that, but yeah." She finally finishes her waffles. She's the slowest eater I have ever met in my life. I don't really mind; it just amuses me. "You know," she muses as she sets down her fork, "nobody would take us seriously if we said Santa Claus or something like that was behind it. But everyone's fascinated, and you know that is exactly what they're telling their young kids when asked."

"That's a good point. The guy does look the part, and everyone likes the idea of a Christmas miracle—even if they don't believe it on a practical level." It is pretty cute. If I ever have kids, I know I'll be telling them this crazy story on Christmas.

"But if we try to present the 'Christmas miracle' angle with anything but our tongues firmly in cheek, we'll lose all credibility." She tries to distract herself with a drink of coffee, but her mug is empty, and she sets it down with a disappointed look.

"You want more coffee?" I get up, grabbing my mug. She nods, and I grab hers, too, and go to fill it from the urn. Two cups in and I'm starting to feel properly awake, but she's still got a glaze to her eyes.

When I make it back to the table, I'm absolutely sure she's watching Jack. The strength of my reaction shocks me; I almost drop one of the mugs. I strengthen my grip just in time, but a few droplets scald my fingers as I set the mugs down.

"What are you looking at?" The words come out sharp and angry before I can stop them.

She looks up with a shocked expression—and with her cheeks full of color. "Sorry, what?"

"You're staring at Jack Whitman again." I lower myself into my seat, doing my best to keep my voice quiet and my tone less... pissy. *She's not mine anymore.* That phrase is really starting to become more like a mantra.

"I'm not staring at him," she snaps back defensively. "I'm trying to figure out how he fits into all this."

I've blown it already, and I know that, but I still can't let it go. "No, seriously. Every time I look over at you I catch you watching the guy. What's going on here?"

"Nothing." Andi's hand shakes slightly as she lifts the mug. Her cheeks are pink and she is avoiding my gaze.

I know what it means, coming from her. And I'm jealous as hell.

"Andi, sweetie, the guy's a player. What are you doing?" Her cheeks go redder, which makes me angrier—and that embarrasses me because I'm not supposed to be jealous right now, or angry, and I know it. And that just pisses me off more.

"Look, his being cute and charming isn't relevant right now. I'm trying to figure out if we're focusing on the wrong suspect," she says simply. "Jack's more of a showman: more energetic and certainly more agile. I also suspect he has more friends among the younger set than his dad. In that sense, he would have an easier time pulling this off." Then her eyes narrow. "What are *you* doing?"

It's like a slap in the face. I know she's trying to hide her interest in Jack—but maybe she's also trying to ignore the subject. She could be shifting the focus of her interest from getting into his pants to getting to the truth about him. *I should trust her.*

Besides, it's her life, not our life. "Nothing." The coffee's too hot; it scalds my throat as I swallow it down.

She stares at me…and then her eyebrows go up and a teasing smirk curves her lips. "Are you getting jealous of one of our subjects there, Dave?"

I snort. It's really pretty tough to stay pissed off at her. "I'm not jealous."

"Coulda' fooled me." Her lips quirk, and the teasing expression leaves her face. "Seriously, David, the guy might be eye candy, but so what? You stared at Gabby's ass almost constantly when she was showing us up to our room, and you didn't hear me complaining."

Now her voice has an edge to it, and my ears start to prickle as my anger melts. *Oh yeah. Gabby.*

The desk clerk, a petite blonde with a tight little skier's body, was a welcome sight after driving up from New York City.

And I sure did get an eyeful as she was leading us up to our room. I just forgot that Andi would probably notice.

"Okay, okay," I concede, backing down a little reluctantly. "I'm not a hypocrite. And I wonder about Jack's involvement in all this, too. I've also got a lot of unanswered questions about him and his dad in general."

Am I salvaging the conversation? I think I am. But deep down, I can still feel that bit of honest jealousy simmering away, making me wary every time she looks in Jack's direction.

"That's fair enough. I do, too. In fact, I wonder about a lot of people in this town. I'm still not sure how so many of them can be treating this...phenomenon like it's just business as usual."

She takes a swallow of coffee and looks over as a new family comes through the glassed-in lobby beside the breakfast room. I follow her glance as the family of four moves in a huddle toward the reception desk.

Mom, dad, older son, and tiny daughter—all with dark, thick hair, and enormous, liquid brown eyes. Definitely up down the coast: their coats are brand new and too light for this weather. They look stunned by the cold they just stepped out of, like cats doused in icy water.

Andi's still on track, talking about the locals. "It's Upstate New York. Even when it's ten degrees out and the snow is up to your thighs, you still have to dig the car out and get to work. Same as when you're neck deep in tourists, I guess." She turns back to me, her shoulders set less stiffly.

Things are relaxing again. I'm actually glad. I'll be happier when we reach some hypothesis about the mistletoe, so then we can finally go back home.

Home: where it's ten degrees warmer on average, with clear streets and my nice, warm penthouse apartment and an underground garage giving me very little need to slog through snow; where I'll have a little breathing room from Andi—which I'm starting to need, if I'm not allowed to touch her—and best of all, no Jack.

I really don't like that guy. I don't think I should be jealous of him, but I still wouldn't have a drink with him willingly. And it's not just because Andi likes him. Really.

She sits back, her chair creaking slightly. "Okay, so. Let's check out that window and then try and get Jack's help in pinning down his dad." She sounds a little steadier and the sadness from her earlier daydreaming is out of her eyes, at least.

I'll take it—though the mention of having to deal with Jack again doesn't excite me.

I get up somewhat abruptly, once our plates and mugs are both empty. "Let's get moving then. I don't know how long your Lothario there is gonna be on the street."

5

ANDI

I'm pretty relieved when David gets up. It was getting awkward, sitting there at the table. I can feel the strain between us, and it exhausts me. Breakfast started out so nice...and then he brought up Jack.

Knock it off. Don't play blame games. We're just stressed from being in close contact for too long. It's messing with his head. Mine, too.

One of the ways that he and I have kept our friendship and partnership together for so many years, even after our marriage collapsed, is to not spend too much time together in one stretch. Between the awkwardness, the sexual tension, and the regrets, it can be tough to deal with. Here in Phoenicia though, we've had no choice but to be close, and it has gotten a little uncomfortable here and there.

I'm still slightly distracted by my thoughts of David and my problematic attraction to Jack when we make our way out into the small lobby. Jack is outside calmly bending over the window glass drawing something in the frost with his finger. I turn my head to look at him, and the doorbell jingles as it's pushed open just as we reach it.

It's Gabby, looking entirely too cute and perky in her matching pink snowsuit, boots, and mittens, like a single scoop of strawberry ice cream rolling out of a freezer. She stops in the doorway as David pauses to step aside for her, and gifts him with a dazzling smile. I fold my arms across my chest, feeling a stab of jealousy that digs deeper every time I see him with her.

Some of that goddamned mistletoe is hanging over them—over all three of us, pretty much. I freeze, indecision mixed with jealousy and my stubborn reluctance to be pushed into anything all roiling around inside of me.

"Hey, good morning, Dave!" Gabby leans up and kisses him on the cheek before he can react.

And then he does—by turning toward her and trying to steal a real kiss. Right in fucking front of me.

My eyes widen and my fists clench. *Oh, you did not just start playing games like that,* I think furiously, even as Gabby slips away from him before he can get what he wants. There's a coy smile on her face as she shakes her head at him and moves back to her post.

Neither one of them so much as looks in my direction. In fact, I may as well not even be there. He just follows her with his gaze. Me, I stifle the urge to elbow him in his side—or maybe his obvious boner—and push my way outside.

The icy day digs a million tiny teeth into my exposed skin, and I'm almost glad to feel it cool me, because on the inside, I feel like I might just burn a hole in the snow with every step.

I barely even look at Jack, and he gets jealous as hell. But then he goes and pulls this right in front of me? How is that fair?

This feels like the world's most passive-aggressive lover's tiff, and that pisses me off even more, because we're not lovers. We probably should never have been lovers at all. But this level of escalation by Dave is just plain rude, even if we were just friends who didn't have any emotional sore spots.

It's been years, and he's never done anything like this before, I think feverishly, worried. How in the world can he be this callous? And how in the world can I still be this vulnerable to anything he does?

I'm blinking back tears as I step out onto the icy sidewalk, the tiny droplets feeling like they might freeze on my lashes. I'm just turning to walk down the street when a firm hand reaches out to grasp my forearm.

My heart lifts slightly with relief. It must be David realizing he is being an idiot and catching up to apologize. *Okay. Maybe I won't throw a snowball at his face just yet.*

I stop and turn—and it's Jack, smiling slyly. He smells like a ski slope—frosty pines and wood smoke. "That was rather rude of your partner," he purrs. Without giving me even a moment to respond, his smile widens and his eyes narrow in invitation as he points a long finger straight up.

I look up slowly...and see an enormous wad of mistletoe dangling from a lamppost over our heads. *Oh shit.*

My cheeks burn as I look back at him—just in time for his lips to come in contact with mine for a kiss I was barely expecting. I freeze, absolutely stunned.

It's not unlike any of the other mistletoe kisses between strangers and acquaintances that I've witnessed regularly since being here. He hasn't even wrapped an arm around me; it's really not very dramatic as far as kisses go. Externally, anyway.

Inside, however, the simple brush of Jack Whitman's lips against mine sends a hard jolt of pleasure through me and leaves me as wobbly as a teen with her first crush. *Oh my God.*

He ends the kiss and moves on as if nothing happened. Meanwhile, I'm standing there as still as a statue just staring after him. His gentle chuckle drifts back toward me over his shoulder, and I simply can't move. My heart is thundering in my ears so hard that when David catches up to me and says something, I can't even hear it.

I turn my head to look at him and see him scowling at me. "What?" I mumble with irritation, in no mood for anymore of whatever soap opera he's trying to turn this into.

"You looked like you were enjoying that kiss," he repeats loudly and slowly, eyebrows drawn down with anger.

I just...stare at him, incredulously. "Actually the whole thing caught me by surprise, thanks. And you were the one trying to turn a peck on the cheek into full on face-sucking with Gabby not two minutes ago!"

His belligerent look crumbles and he backs off slightly. I glare at him and then turn to see where Jack wandered off to. He's strolling down the street, getting further away from us with every second.

"I'm going to catch up with our subject. You stay here and sulk if you want." Without a second look at David, I turn and hurry after Jack, going as fast as I can trust my boots to take me on the ice-coated sidewalk. *With all the extra money coming in, you'd think they would spend a bit on extra bags of salt!*

"Wait!" I call after Jack. He comes to a stop and looks back over his shoulder, a look of bemusement on his face.

He turns to face me as I wobble up. "If you're wanting another kiss, you should at least buy me a drink first," he advises. I draw up short, blinking at him, so at a loss that he bursts out laughing and shakes his head. "I'm kidding! What can I do for you?"

"I need your help," I say simply, worried that I'll start stammering if I even try to discuss that kiss. Although...it was still very, very noteworthy. I haven't had very many kisses that have left me trembling and breathless, like I'd just swept down a slope in a toboggan.

He lifts an eyebrow. "Me? Oh, well then. What are the details, Miss Andromeda?"

"It's just Andi. I need your help nailing down an interview with your father within the next two days. Three tops? We have to move on after that, and our investigation just won't be complete without a word from him."

He winces slightly. "I can't make any promises, unfortunately. I wish I could. Your work really does fascinate me. But my father, as you have no doubt learned, is notoriously hard to pin down."

"Jack, please." I draw a bit closer to him. He must have a very well-insulated coat; I couldn't feel much warmth coming off of him when he leaned against me to kiss me. And I feel nothing coming off him now. "I hate being pushy, but we're in a tight spot here."

He strokes his slightly pointed chin. I can hear David belatedly puffing up behind me, and I ignore him. Jack's brilliant blue eyes flick over to David and then back to my face. "How so?"

"Everything points to your father's involvement. And yours, for that matter." I stare back at him as he smirks at me. "Say what you want, but you know it's true. You and your dad are the two biggest Christmas enthusiasts that either of us has ever seen."

"Winter enthusiast, in my case, not just Christmas. Really, holidays are far more his bag, especially this one. But go on." His eyes are twinkling at me like he thinks this is all a very funny joke.

"In the end, I don't want to do anything either of you isn't comfortable with. But you cannot pull an event—or prank, or whatever you want to call it—this big, so big that it makes national news, and expect people not to be curious about how you pulled it off." I can't keep the plea out of my voice.

He stares at me almost neutrally, just a gleam of humor in his eyes, neither confirming nor denying his involvement. Again. "Regardless of who is behind this and what method was used, I still don't understand. How will knowing the specifics of Phoenicia's little miracle help anyone?" he asks cryptically.

I blink up at him, wrapping my coat more closely around me. The cold seems to be cutting through it more sharply with every gust of wind. *This exact coat saw me through a Canadian winter. Why can't it handle this?* "What do you mean?"

"Some things are fueled by belief, not by facts, my dear. Many of the best experiences in life have little to do with logic." He looks past me again at David. "Take romance, for example."

"What about it?" David grits out through clenched teeth. I feel my blood pressure rise, but I don't confront him. Getting the interview is too important.

"Well," Jack says mildly, as I struggle to keep warm and find myself failing. "People do not fall in love because they present each other with a list of logical arguments why they are a good and compatible choice, though they might try to come up with one to justify their choice.

"But that," he continues with a widening smile, "is something humans come up with entirely after the fact. Our hearts make the decision before our brains can kick in—or sometimes, in spite of what our brains think. And we must simply trust that the one we love is worthy of our devotion.

"Love is irrational, my friends, and though it must make sense to us, we base much of it on faith. And it is the same with miracles—even silly little ones like this." He winks.

I'm so cold. I need to duck back inside and get some more coffee into me before we take one single step further down the street. "We're paranormal investigators, Jack. We're here to try to make sense of things. I understand that you think removing the mystery will remove the magic from the situation—"

"Yes, I absolutely do," he replies mildly. "Take out too much of the mystery and you remove the wonder." He seems to notice my shivering, and a concerned line appears between his brows, but he doesn't comment on it yet.

"What makes you think that our investigation has that kind of power? Jack, look. We will probably write a book and also present to a convention or two on this, which will mean even more tourists and more positive attention for your town. Unless we end up with conclusive proof either way, all that David and I can do in the end is present the evidence, and let people draw their own conclusions." Talking so much seems suddenly exhausting. I'm shivering harder and harder.

David steps up beside me finally, giving me a glance that actually looks concerned. "I think what Andi's trying to say is, no matter what evidence is presented, some people will always believe, and even those who don't will probably enjoy it anyway. And their kids will believe, because it's a great little story. If we ever have kids, I'll tell them this one myself."

We? Hold the fucking phone! Everything goes screeching to a halt inside of me, and I start shivering harder.

That was a Freudian slip, I tell myself firmly. And of course, it was—but I still stand there with my heart pounding, wondering if David is aware of what he just said. He doesn't seem to be. He just stays focused on the conversation.

"That's interesting," Jack murmurs. "So, what you are saying is, no matter whether you actually reveal what happened, or lead people in entirely the wrong direction, you think people will simply take the details you've provided and draw their own conclusions?"

Jack sounds incredulous—like it never occurred to him that we wouldn't actually be out here trying to dissect a Christmas miracle and to change everyone's minds. We're not here to take the magic out of Christmas. Just determine whether there is any.

"That's it exactly," I say in a tiny, shivery voice, and both men turn to me with almost identical frowns of concern. "Informing people is not the same as telling them what to think. I'm sorry if I made you think we were here to...debunk Phoenicia's miracle.

That was never the aim. We're chasing *wonder* up here. David kicks the tires on everything we do, but in the end, that's only so that we can have something that stands up to real debunkers."

I shift my weight, feeling a little wobbly, and am completely surprised when David grabs my arm to steady me. Catching Jack's eye, I repeat, "Please. Just an interview, so we have something to wrap this investigation up."

"I'll ask my father directly and then call you," he replies, suddenly looking very troubled. "I'm very sorry about this. Perhaps you should go back inside and warm up."

"Sorry for what?" I manage to ask a moment before my knees buckle.

"Whoa!" David catches me and steadies me with surprising ease. "Okay, yeah, let's get you back inside." He bends down and tosses me effortlessly over his shoulder. "Give us a call later," he yells over my body and starts heading back to the bed and breakfast.

"What the hell is wrong with you?" The edge in his voice is gone, replaced only with concern. He moves me down his torso, so he's cradling me like a baby instead of marching me around like a sack of potatoes.

I drag my head up, barely able to meet his gaze. I'm numb, inside and out. The wind feels like it's found a way through my clothes, skin, flesh...right through to my bones, coating them in a layer of ice.

"I'm so cold," I mumble softly and then look up at him, astonished by how scared that suddenly makes me. I've only been outside maybe ten minutes. But I feel like I've been wandering around a mountainside without my coat. "Help."

"Okay, sweetheart, okay," he mutters as we turn up the walk. "Let's get you inside and get a hot drink into you. Did your feet get wet or something?"

"I don't know. I was just standing there..." My words are going away again. I feel a fluffy haze closing in over my vision like frost over a window. "I just got so cold."

The blast of warm air as we step into the inn stings my skin, and I let out a little sob of relief. He leads me in through the lobby and sits me on the bench. "Hey, can we get a cup of coffee over here?" he calls out to Gabby.

She jumps up off her stool, staring at me worriedly. "She get a chill?"

"Yeah, it came on pretty suddenly. I figured we'd try a hot drink." He gives her a tight business-smile, all hint of flirtation gone.

"Okay, yeah. Hang on." She hurries into the breakfast room and comes back with a steaming cup for both of us. "You think you're going to need help getting her up the stairs?"

I'm a little shocked. Did I misread Gabby? "I can get up the stairs," I insist. And I damn well will. "Just give me a few minutes."

I swallow down the coffee greedily, feeling a faint burn on my tongue but not caring. I need the warmth. But a few moments after taking the last gulp, I blink my eyes open and look around in confusion.

The warmth spreads inside of me...and then gutters out like a match struck in an Arctic wind. *Fuck. What is this? Am I going to end up in the damn hospital like that biker?*

"Let's...just go upstairs," I say through chattering teeth.

6

DAVID

I try to keep my cool as I help Andi up the stairs. She's shivering so hard that it's actually freaking me out. I don't want her to end up in the hospital because the wind chill factor left her hypothermic.

But if I can't get her stable and warmed up in the next hour, the hospital is exactly where we're going. I tell her this, quietly but firmly, on the way up the stairs. "And then we're going home, sweetheart. We can do a phone interview with Whitman from my penthouse, damn it, with the heat cranked up to eighty."

"We can't give up now," she protests quietly. I scoff.

"We damn well can and will, if it comes down to it. There's no way I'm letting you end up hurt for the sake of another book. You're too important. Now come on, let's get you up the rest of these stairs." I help her up the last few steps and then down the hall, where Gabby has unlocked the door and is busily bringing carafes of coffee, cocoa, and hot water with a basket of teas.

I feel a brief flash of embarrassment as she steps aside so I can help Andi through the door. She doesn't even meet my eyes. Apparently, I read a whole hell of a lot more into that kiss she gave me than she had intended, and I don't have the time or energy to live that down.

Stupid. And I know it upset Andi. That was why she went barreling ahead of me into the street, straight into a kiss with Jack that then pissed me off in turn. And then, somehow, this happened.

That's the really horrible part; I don't quite know how she ended up getting this chilled through. She wasn't even on the street a quarter of an hour. She was properly bundled and her hair wasn't wet. How did this happen?

"Thank you," I tell Gabby on her way out as I help Andi over to the edge of the bed. She's shivering and huffing even in the warm room. *Very bad sign.*

"What the hell happened? You're shaking like you were out there for hours." I help her out of her coat, which feels perfectly dry...but when I touch her bare wrist in the process, it feels like she had it resting in a bucket of ice.

"I don't know," she chatters, peeling off her gloves to reveal almost colorless hands. "I feel horrible. I'm scared."

She hugs herself and hunches forward as she sits on the edge of the bed, and I hastily pour her some cocoa and bring it over. "Here," I tell her, and help her hold the cup so she can swallow the contents without sloshing it everywhere.

"I'm so cold," she mumbles. She swallows down the cocoa so fast that I fear she's burned her throat, but all she does is shake her head and push the mug back at me. "It barely makes a dent. I need more."

"Okay. I'm gonna suggest you take your clothes off and get under the covers," I say quickly, trying to ignore just how much this is freaking me out.

This is a million times worse than watching her get kissed by another guy. She's *suffering*. I'd rather lose a limb than watch and do nothing.

She nods and starts peeling off her layers of sweaters, her hat and scarf, her boots. The skin beneath is so very pale, even for her. I lay a hand against her cheek and the chill there stings me. "Okay, sweetie, this isn't good," I mutter. "If we can't get you warmed up, I'm driving you to the hospital."

She looks up at me bleakly as she strips down to her long underwear. I check the sleeve cuff to find that it's not damp either. It should be insulating. But she's still sitting here with her teeth chattering.

"Please, no goddamn hospital," she mumbles. "You know how much I hate them."

"Yeah, and you know how much I hate the idea of you risking your health if it turns out you *need* a hospital." I keep my voice gentle, but with an edge to it, because *Goddamn it, Andi.* "I'm giving this half an hour, and if you don't start improving, off we go."

She stares at me, her eyes starting to go bright, and her chin starting to tremble. *Oh shit,* I think, feeling a familiar panic try to fight past my control. I squash it, reminded again that I still love this woman, even if I can never be with her.

But then, before I can say anything reassuring, she bursts into tears.

Shit shit shit. Okay. Calm down, man. "Fuck. Okay. Andi, honey, what can I do to help you?"

"I don't know," she sobs, sounding disoriented and a little hysterical. "I'm so cold and I can't think, but please, no hospital. People go there to die!"

It hits me, even as I scoop her up and help her get bundled into bed. She cries softly the whole time, mumbling "no hospital" as my heart sinks into my boots.

Of course she's scared of hospitals. She doesn't even want to explore abandoned ones for ghosts anymore. How much of her family has gone into a hospital in the last five years and never come out?

Her parents: car accident. Her grandmother: cancer. A cousin to suicide. Her favorite aunt who had gone in for appendicitis: dead two weeks later from sepsis. That last one, Andi had gone to the hospital every day and camped there as much as they would let her, just so Aunt Margaret wouldn't be alone.

It's only been two years, so of course she still feels wary.

She sits up in a ball against the pillows while I wrap the blankets and comforters around her, and then turn on the heated mattress pad I got her as a Christmas present.

"Okay," I tell her, breathless but steady. "We are going to get you warmed up and rested, and once you're feeling better, we're going to do absolutely no legwork that does not take place in a heated car or a heated building."

She nods, sniffling and shivering, her cheeks still coated with tears. "O-okay."

Damn this cold. And damn me for not noticing sooner that something was wrong with Andi, all because I was too busy driving another wedge between us from jealousy.

And damn Jack—just for being Jack. And maybe for being more interesting than me.

I peel off my outerwear and get everything hung up while we wait for her to warm up. I bring her chamomile tea and check in halfway through her gulping it down; she's still pale and cold, but the terrified look is weakening. Satisfied for the moment, I pull off my boots, noticing that the chunks of snow on them are still intact.

"How the fuck do any people live up here year-round?" I grumble as I put the boots on the doormat. Being willing to deal with this every day seems completely crazy to me.

No answer from Andi, but at least she's stopped crying. I grab half a cup of coffee, fill the rest with cocoa and walk over to see how she's doing again.

She's drained her mug of tea and set it aside, burrowing so

deep down into the blankets that she looks like a pile of bedding with a face. "How you feeling?" I ask her softly, wondering if I should be encouraged or worried by her sudden quiet.

She blinks up at me, and then says softly, "It's only a little better."

I check my watch. "A little is better than nothing. We've only been up here ten minutes." I told myself I'd give it twenty more before I really need to worry, and it hasn't been that long. *Maybe it will be okay.*

"I'm not leaving you alone until I know you're all right and don't need a hospital," I say firmly. "I know we've had a rough time being in such close quarters for so long, but this is too important. We'll both just have to deal with it."

I don't just mean the mess with Gabby, or the mess with Jack, or the sexual tension between us—which I know she's been feeling, too. Those are concerns, though now is really not the time to think about it.

It's hard to get out of my head, though. Through the door separating our rooms, I've heard her moaning at night. I even heard her cry out my name—and that was sweet hell to listen to.

I'm putting it all aside. Sexual tension and relationship problems can wait. The squabble that drove us out into the cold seems pointless and silly now. "Okay?"

She nods and then her face crumples. "Thank you."

I want to hug her so badly that my hands flex at my sides, but I force myself to simply smile. I drag over a chair, so I can sit next to her. "No problem."

I miss the feel of her in my arms so fiercely right now that I can barely stand it. But all I can do is care for her in the ways that she will allow.

She's the one who set the boundaries. It's up to her whether to take them down or not. I wish I had understood that better back when we were together.

It's yet another thing that I wish I could show her. That I've changed. That I'm not that same kid I was then, the one who disappointed her so much.

Hell, I think we've both figured out by now that it's almost impossible to keep a relationship together in any real way when your prefrontal lobe hasn't even finished forming. If I had realized that back then, I would have waited years before even trying to get with her.

I still hope I can. I know it's stupid of me to camp at her gates like this. I've done everything I can to hide it. But I'm the kind of guy who can't hide anything for shit.

"You know, if Jack can get us that interview, that's all we have left to do, and maybe monitoring the mistletoe on the fifth." I try to distract her from her discomfort and fear by talking like the future beyond her current reality is a foregone conclusion. "Then we can just go home."

She seems to have thawed out enough to at least talk shop a little, but it takes her a minute. "Do you think anyone will mess with the deer cams if we put them up around town?"

"Not if we get permission from the shopkeepers. If this follows the pattern we expected," I see Andi reach for her mug, and I get up to fill it with more tea, "then we will see all the mistletoe either disappear or be taken down between sundown and sunup on the last of the Twelve Days."

"The fifth." She frowns hazily, then sighs at herself and nods.

"Exactly." I bring it back to her and our fingers brush. Hers are still cold. I frown as I feel them barely close around the warm mug, and gently wrap my hands around her own to help her grasp it. "Come on, sweetheart, you can do this. Don't spill."

"If I keep putting more fluid in me I'll end up freezing to death on the toilet," she chatters out, and then lets out a high, nervous giggle. "Especially with all the caffeine."

"One of the reasons I switched to decaf," I joke in a dry tone, and she lets out a tiny laugh that sounds like a sob. "But I can't have you pissing icicles. We've got to warm you up a little first."

She covers her face with her hands, and her shoulders shake. I hold the mug for her until she calms down and help her sip at it. She takes her time, and I wonder if her burned tongue is finally starting to hurt or if she's too numb still to feel it.

"There you go," I say when the mug is dry. I set it aside and lean over to catch her eye. "Are you thawing out?"

She takes a deep breath—and then starts to shiver again, wrapping her arms around herself. "I still can't get warm," she whimpers.

It's been twenty-five minutes. She seems a little better, and she's begging me not to go to the hospital. But I'm so alarmed by how pale and cold and shivery she is, even with blankets bundled and heat applied, that I'm still half tempted to carry her down to the car. If I do that, though, she'll probably never forgive me.

Shit.

"Well, look. I only have one other thing I can try, but I'm afraid you'll throw pillows at me when you recover."

I shouldn't even be thinking about this. It's a stupid idea. But it's pretty much always recommended in situations like this: body heat.

With as few clothes as possible.

"What are you gonna do?" she mumbles, her eyes alarmingly dull.

That expression on her face decides it for me. I start unbuckling my belt.

7

ANDI

Whoa, hey wait a minute. The chill that has permeated my body leaves me hazy, but I'm not so far out of it to not feel the shock when David starts shucking off his jeans.

I see red wool flannel underneath, and then he stretches up and strips off his sweaters and shirt as well. Standing there in his bright red long johns, he's a weird mix of sexy and ridiculous, which perfectly fits the sudden strip-down. "The fuck?" I mumble.

Are we boning for warmth now? I have to pause a moment to sort out how I feel about that. My emotions are mixed, to say the least. I never stopped feeling that spark of attraction, but I never stopped feeling the wariness and frustration either.

I decide to hold off on getting annoyed until I know what the hell is actually up. Meanwhile, my gaze is taking a walk up and down his body before I even realize it.

He's filled out a little since our days together, in a nice, defined way that makes the flannel stretch flatteringly over his limbs and chest. I wonder if his hipbones would still end up leaving bruises on my thighs. Then I tear my mind out of the gutter as fast as I find it there. *Shit.*

He grins awkwardly. "Uh, well, the only way I have left to help you warm up is me. Unless you feel that having me sink you in a hot bath might do the trick." His voice is so gentle, his eyes worried. I know that we would probably already be halfway to the hospital by now if he had his way.

I'm glad that he hasn't pushed the issue yet. "And that means that I spend the next couple hours..."

"Naked and wet in front of me. Yeah. Awkward." Did the crotch of his ridiculous underwear just gain some volume at the thought? I'm too numb to smile or blush right now.

"Yeah, that's g-gonna be too awkward. Let's...let's try this instead," I stammer, my whole body aching from shivering so long.

This has to work. And really, I'll take a cuddle right now—gladly. My muscles hurt, my joints hurt, and my skin stings from the contrast between the warm environment and the cold that seems to have seeped into my bones.

I started getting cold after Jack kissed me, I realize. But that has to be a coincidence. It's not like his lips—which weren't particularly cold—had somehow given me hypothermia. The kiss just came so soon after I went outside that I somehow connected the two events in my head.

Everything that David has done for me has helped a little, enough that I'm not quite so scared or cold any more. But as he takes hold of the covers to slip into the spot beside me for the first time in years, my stomach flips over nervously.

He lifts the edge of the covers and climbs in next to me—a welcome presence that I have to pretend to only tolerate. But then I realize I can't simply tolerate it. The moment his leg brushes against mine, the warmth of his body starts to sink into me...and stays.

I let out a gasp and cuddle against him at once, jamming my cheek against his shoulder. It's not my imagination. *Oh holy crap.* I close my eyes, basking in the heat coming off of his sleek, hard body even through the flannel.

"Whoa, hey," he laughs awkwardly as he gets settled, wrapping the bedding around us both and then looping an arm around my shoulders. The warmth coming off of him feels similar to when he turned on the mattress pad, but the heat sinks in more deeply, and it doesn't feel like it's fading away faster than it gets to me.

"Don't make fun. You're warm," I complain, though I'm starting to notice an ache inside me that has nothing to do with the cold. I missed cuddling with him.

For all the flaws in our relationship, he was always loved to cuddle, and I liked it, too. Now I remember how good it feels to have his long limbs wrapped around me, and his cheek against the top of my head. My eyes clench further shut, as if I can use pressure alone to keep the sudden, wistful tears from escaping.

He's gone very quiet. I can feel his heart beating fast against my hand. His chest heaves; his breath shivers. I have no doubt that if I slid my hand about two feet south, I'd feel his pulse pounding hard somewhere else, too.

I shouldn't be thinking about David's cock. He's got a really nice one—big and thick, always promising more satisfaction than it ever gave me. But really, like the rest of him, it's not my business anymore.

There came a time when signs of his affection or arousal put me on edge instead of enticing or exciting me. They told me of his expectations, while warning me as well that my own would probably not be met. At that time, I started to tense up whenever I saw the signs, knowing that, at best, I'd have to put up with more awkward sex, or at worst, we'd end up arguing.

Now, though, as I lean against him and soak up his warmth,

my eyes closed, I feel the tremors inside of me go still and my muscles slowly unlock. "Oh my God," I mumble.

"Any better?" He sounds hopeful—and a little breathless. His grip tightens around me, and another wave of warmth runs through my body.

"Yes," I gasp, more surprised than anything. "You were right about this one, okay? You can make fun of me later." I look into his eyes briefly and tighten my grip on him. I feel him squirm happily, his heartbeat picking up again.

I'm trying not to let it get to me. He's probably saving my life right now—or at least saving me from a night in my least favorite place in the world. But I know that the circle of his arms is dangerous territory for me.

Still, I'm not going to complain. Not one bit. Not even if I end up having to fight the whole night to ignore how much I'm enjoying this.

He reaches over and folds his hands around one of mine, touching me experimentally. A thoughtful look deepens on his face even as a shiver goes through him. "It's working," he sighs finally, but makes no move to let my hand go.

I don't let his go either. I lean my head against his chest instead and close my eyes as his heartbeat slowly evens out. I know he has to be wishing we were doing more than just cuddling; there's part of me that wishes that, too, which is why it's dangerous.

"Sorry about this," I sigh as feeling comes prickling back uncomfortably into my fingers and toes. "I know you want to get out of here, and here we are spending an extra day because my ass got a chill."

"Well, the mistletoe phenomenon will end when it ends, regardless. I can put the damn deer cams up myself if I have to." He's stroking my hair. He's not supposed to do that. And I'm not supposed to be leaning into it, eyes half-closed like a contented cat.

But here we are.

"We'll catch whatever there is to catch on them the night of the fifth, and then move the hell on the next day, regardless. Our Phoenician Father Christmas can talk to you over the phone if he can't see you before you feel better." His tone is firm but calm, and I sigh through my nose and simply nod my agreement.

"How are you feeling now?" he asks me as he keeps petting me. I should protest. I should definitely complain.

I stretch against him, feeling a shiver go through him that has nothing to do with cold. I smile against his chest, feeling powerful and strangely calm about it. I still get to decide how far this goes.

There's something about that that is so satisfying—and tempting as well. We could stay here cuddling all day if I want, and he'll be happy to do it. Or we could do...more. And I *know* David would be happy to do that.

No pressure. None. It's all up to me.

"This is nice," I murmur wholeheartedly.

He goes very still for a little while as he digests this. Then he smiles a little. "Yeah?"

"Yeah." I stifle a yawn. Now that I'm not sitting there shivering from both my dropping temperature and my fear of a looming hospital visit, I'm absolutely drained of energy. The caffeine from the drinks isn't even touching me.

My muscles ache. My body, warm again, has gone slack from loss of tension. My joints pop as my body settles. I can't keep my eyes open.

"Dunno if I'll be conscious long, but I'm not feeling like I'm gonna freeze any more. I'm exhausted though." *What the hell even was that? And why was it that only David's touch could fix me?*

I stifle a yawn as his lean hand slips down to cup my cheek

experimentally. His skin feels slightly cool now, instead of burning hot. "Okay, well, you're warm again. But I think I'd better stick around for a while."

I should argue. But I know he's not pushing the issue so much as he's enduring the situation and forcing himself to hold me and go no further. It would make me feel guilty...but how many times have I wished he would show some self-control?

He's showing it now, and it fascinates me. If I wasn't so damned worn out, I just might want to test his resolve. *Or maybe give him permission to give in.* "Thank you," I mumble finally, as I slip gently off to sleep.

The Christmas snowstorm never ended. The snow just kept piling up outside, until now. I can see the tops of the drifts level with the second-floor window. We're trapped.

The lights are on. The room is warm. There's food downstairs. The water runs. We're safe—but we're not going anywhere.

And neither one of us cares right now. We're tangled up, kissing.

Time blurs past with the easy cross-fade of a movie. No awkwardness. No talking.

I'm pinning him down, despite his superior size and strength. Maybe he's letting me, but it doesn't matter. In the end, I'm driving.

And somehow, we're both loving it.

He can't speak anymore. His whole body is taut under me, muscles tight, the cords in his neck standing out as he throws his head back. Small grunts of pleasure escape him as I ride his rigid cock, setting the pace.

"Hold still," I order him, bearing down on him from above as my thighs straddle his hips. "Don't push. Don't you dare bust yet."

He stares up at me in fascination, his broad chest heaving, his eyes glazed in shock, and his body beaded with sweat. I've been riding him long enough that my knees crack. I barely notice the pain over the burning ache of need between my thighs.

His back arches, and he strains under me, his body fighting his will as he starts to tremble and pant. "Not yet," *I whisper in his ear, and his breath grows harsher, the restraint exciting him perversely.*

I feel the airy, floating heat between my thighs, a sense of generic euphoria expanding there in the absence of a climax. Dreams come from memories, after all, and I have no memory of orgasm. I just hear myself gasping "Yes...yes!" as poor David starts to go wild under me.

*I grind away roughly on him, blissed out as he grunts and lets out deep, sharp cries. It almost sounds like he's in pain, as if I'm stabbing him with every thrust. I feel his back arch under me...*and I pop awake into my brightly lit room at the bed and breakfast.

Shit.

It takes me a few moments to get my bearings. My whole body is tingly and warm now, misted with sweat under my long johns. The terrifying cold is a fading memory.

The feel of David's cock inside of me as I ride him stays sharp in my mind as I catch my breath.

I can feel fabric stretched against my fingertips and realize that I've dug my nails into the flannel covering David's forearm. My lungs burn as I pant for air like I've just run a marathon. He's relaxed, even with me curled against his side, and he blinks awake drowsily, apparently not noticing my almost bruising grip as I relax it.

"You okay?" he murmurs drowsily, not even really focused on me yet. "Think you called out in your sleep."

"Yeah...yeah," I murmur as I lift my head to look him in the face. "Good dreams. Bad timing, but good dreams." *Sort of. I liked them, but I can't do anything about them.*

He grins drowsily. "Oh really?"

"Oh yeah." I shift my weight—and feel my body start to wake up as well. Tingling, I lift my head from his chest and lean back to look at him.

Our eyes meet. He strokes his hand back over my braid, and then cups the back of my skull and leans down to kiss me.

We're both half awake. Our lips brush and a delightful tremor runs all the way through me. I whimper softly—and do my best not to chase his lips as he moves away.

"S-sorry," he murmurs. "I..."

My head feels too light. The room seems to rock a little, like a cabin on a yacht. "I need to get up," I mutter, and he nods, backing off a little more.

He helps me to the bathroom and I shut myself in, heart banging away in my chest.

Fuck.

8

DAVID

I ended up being saved by the bell—or rather, by the *Tubular Bells* ringtone of my phone telling me that someone related to the current case was calling. It was Jack with an invitation to an early supper later today with himself, his father, and some guests. If, of course, Andi was feeling well enough.

She was and insisted that we take the invitation. And that's how we found ourselves driving out to the Whitman lands just hours after we nearly had to take Andi to the hospital.

"Are you still cold?" I ask her, reminding myself that I should still prioritize that over everything else. It's not the first thing that springs to mind, though. That comes out next, but only after she sits in silence in the passenger seat beside me for almost a minute. "Are you still pissed off at me?"

More silence.

Shit. I hate this. More than being yelled at, more than being cried at, I hate the long, awkward silences that happen when she's really thinking something over. They remind me too much of that uncomfortable hour between when I'd said all that shit I shouldn't have and when she'd walked out.

I'm probably about to say way too much again. But this time, I know that admitting my feelings is the right thing to do. Not the comfortable thing and maybe not the safe thing—for all I know it could totally backfire.

But it's the right and honest thing.

"Look, if you expect me to feel bad because I kissed you, I'm sorry, because I don't. I really do not, and I don't regret waking up with you in my arms either."

That gets me a glare...but then her face softens. She's still quiet, though.

"Andi..." I trail off, going quiet myself as I navigate past a particularly sharp turn in the road. The Whitmans live high up the mountain, so high that they sit across the valley from the ski resort. Driving there takes focus in this snowy mess.

As soon as it's back to the bland climb through the woods, I go on. "I can recognize that you want me to keep my distance and keep things as they have been these past year, with us just being friendly. I can even respect your wishes and do it—most of the time.

"But if I kiss you first thing when I wake up, I can't feel bad about it. It's what I have wished I could do for years. I can't turn off how good it feels."

There. Now it's out there. It might've come out a bit angrier than it should have. And it was maybe even a bit gentler than my angry self wanted it to be. Maybe it means the end of our relationship; I just don't know.

"I need a minute," she finally says, a touch of pain in her voice. The anticipation is threatening to kill me, but I simply nod and keep driving for a while.

A minute later, I spy a turn-off up ahead, and I start to slow down so I can pull into it smoothly. I notice her sit forward against the seatbelt a little.

"What are you doing?" she asks in a tone of baffled annoyance.

"You said you needed a minute. I gave it to you. Well, now we need to talk about this, and put it to bed enough that we can focus on the damn interview instead of stewing on it all night. Okay? Can we do that?"

She takes a shivery breath. "Fine. But you had better keep the damn heat on."

"Of course."

I pull us into one of the small parking spaces lined up at the inner edge of the turn-off. The view down the mountain is dreary in winter: a slope of bony dormant trees barely broken up by clusters of pine.

Old stone ruins and boundary fences, covered half the year by foliage, are scattered and exposed on the slope like broken teeth. A blanket of snow covers everything, and the blue shadows and pink streaks of the gathering sunset are the only real color in the landscape.

"Look," she says finally, with a tone of tense resignation that tells me I'm not the only one in the car who is taking an emotional risk. "You know I love you. I tried to love you as a friend, but it has never quite worked out. ...and the reason for that is...I never stopped being attracted to you," she admits, shocking the ever-loving hell out of me.

"Wait, what? You never said anything!" I'm too startled to feel angry. The frustration of the last few years doesn't seem quite so huge if it's been shared, even if only in secret.

"I couldn't." She can't look at me right now, but at least she's talking. I let her gather her wits while she stares down at her hands beside me. "I couldn't afford to, not for a long time. Both of us had too much growing to do."

"Well, I'm not gonna argue over that, especially since a lot of that was on my end of things." It's only the ugly truth. I just couldn't face it at the time. "But I'm not the same guy I was at twenty-two, honey."

"You are, but you're not," she murmurs. "I...don't want us going through that terrible relationship drama again. But that's different from not wishing we could..." She goes quiet and shakes her head, dropping her face into her hands.

She's not crying. She is, however, blushing. I watch her quietly until she stops hiding her face.

"You okay?" I ask as she lifts her head. A gust of wind rattles the bare branches outside and sends a dusting of snow to the ground. She nods slowly, but that alarming thoughtfulness is still on her face.

"I'm not entirely the same person either," she says suddenly. "I've got my own regrets. I couldn't seem to figure out that I wasn't the only person in the relationship who was too young to have a clue."

She doesn't sound like she's being charitable. That's one thing about Andi—she too often makes concessions for the sake of keeping the peace. But then again, she's gotten better at standing up for herself in the last few years. I search her expression with my gaze and see only tired earnestness.

"Well, look, obviously we're both still a good team on a lot of levels, or we wouldn't be able to do this work together anymore." I take a deep breath. "I've wanted more than that ever since we broke up. I wanted you—but I knew I wasn't ready to try again."

She goes pale, then the blush comes back, and she has that shy look she gets sometimes when she thinks no one is looking. It's adorable. "I've always been scared that trying again will ruin things between us. It was hard enough recovering the first time—I don't know if we could survive it a second time."

I swallow and turn to look out the windshield. A fat squirrel hops onto the hood of my car and tucks her paws up against her chest, peering in at us hopefully. Her fur is so thick that she doesn't even seem to notice the cold.

"Cute little guy," Andi murmurs warmly, some of the tension broken. The squirrel scrambles off, leaving little paw prints behind. "I never wanted to be just friends. But I thought it was necessary."

"So did I at the time. But does it have to be just friendship forever, when neither of us wants it to be?" I take a deep breath. "I'll deal with it if you say no, but...I have to ask."

That terrible silence again. For a little while I'm absolutely convinced that she's going to say no. But all she says is, "I've got some reservations. I have to guard myself against any more...problems."

"If you guard yourself forever we're always going to be in limbo like this, sweetheart," I protest softly. "Do you think that there's any chance we can try again?"

She turns a soft smile on me, one that's full of a lot more promise than those long, unnerving silences. "I'll think about it," she says, and it doesn't sound like she's putting me off this time.

My heart's light as hell as we make the rest of the drive up the mountain.

"So where did you two meet?" Dr. Whitman asks a little while later as we settle in his study. Dinner isn't quite ready yet —the short delay down the mountain didn't eat up too much time.

I look around the cozy space lined with books and heated by its own fireplace, with an embossed tin ceiling and a wood-inlaid floor. He's stretched out on one of the couches while we take the other, and Jack sits in a wingback chair near us, examining the contents of Andi's gear bag.

The room smells of burning pine logs and the mulled wine we were greeted at the door with. It's been fifteen minutes since that greeting, and so far, it's felt like we're the ones being interviewed.

"We went to school together," Andi says in the calm, cheerful voice she uses when she's being transparent in the hopes of drawing in an interviewee. "We've known each other through our families for...almost two decades now."

She's talking with an awkward little smile on her face suddenly, like she's introducing her boyfriend to an older relative.

He smiles indulgently and nods, squinting with amusement. "So, you were in love all that time?"

"Uh, just friends," I hasten to correct, and she nods quickly and awkwardly.

"Yeah, best friends." She takes a deep breath. "We started investigating paranormal events and locations when I was sixteen."

"Oh, so the love part came later?" His bright blue eyes twinkle at her. I press my lips together and examine the patterns on the ceiling, trying not to let my amusement show. He really has her on the spot. Me too, but I don't have an uncontrollable blush reflex.

She coughs into her fist. "Um—" she starts.

"Dad," Jack warns good-naturedly as he looks up from the camera he's fiddling with. "Be nice. She's had a long day."

His father beams. "Of course. So, you went on your first ghost hunt when you were sixteen?"

It's weird. Normally, around now, I would be holding the camera, and Andi would be asking the questions. But everything's been turned on its ear. I wonder if the Whitmans had planned it that way. I slide my bag out from under my chair and start unpacking the digital audio recorder we use for interviews.

"I'm sorry, young man, but I thought we said no cameras."

Dr. Whitman lifts an eyebrow at me as I pull out the box, which is chunky, gray, and about twice the size of my smartphone.

I look over at his son, who I swear is recording us, and bite back a retort, smiling instead. "It's just the audio recorder, as we discussed."

"Oh!" He laughs a little, taking a swallow of his wine. "I understand. Go on then." He turns his gaze back to Andi, who takes a deep breath before going on.

"Well, I was sixteen, and I had a crush on David, and—"

"Wait, you did?" I turn a stunned look on Andi and hear Jack snicker slightly. "Sorry. Go on?"

"So, when he told me that we would be recording EVPs at an old New England churchyard, I half believed he actually wanted a particularly creepy make-out spot. But instead, we spent the night huddled together listening to ghosts whispering." There's a wistful smile on her face as she reminisces.

I listen in absolute fascination, staring at her as she describes the first night we ever spent together. How she didn't know if I would make a move, and how she'd been trying to figure out what she would do if I didn't. Breathless nervousness. And the whole time, I'd been oblivious—because I was dealing with the exact same thing.

"So, did the ghosts actually talk?" Jack sounds genuinely fascinated.

"Yes, they did," Andi says excitedly.

I smile and speak up, her enthusiasm catching. "One of them said my name. Well, there were some fragments of speech we isolated on the EVP recordings, but the problem was, we had— and still have—no way of proving that they aren't something else. Someone talking, a radio playing in a car passing by the cemetery...the skeptics can always get us on things like that." I admit my frustration quietly.

"That's not the only problem. A lot of the time, we'll experience a seriously intense paranormal experience—poltergeist activity, voices, sounds of knocking, even a sighting of something," Andi shrugs animatedly, "but the batteries on the camera will die. It won't record, and we get nothing to show for it but snow and white noise. Photographs never turn out, either. Almost like something is messing with us."

"That's probably the most frustrating part," I agree. "I'm still a skeptic, but I'm an open-minded skeptic. I want to have that evidence so that I can examine it and have real proof. But I'd estimate we end up being able to use maybe a quarter of what we end up collecting."

"Yeah, that's even a little generous," Andi sighs, reaching over to squeeze my hand.

I almost drop the recorder.

"Uh…yeah." *Stop that, sweetheart, otherwise I'm gonna have to do this interview while hiding an awkward boner—oh, shit. Too late.* I squirm slightly in my seat and set the too-small-to-hide-anything recorder on my lap.

"And yet you keep trying." Dr. Whitman sits back, meshing his fingers over his belly. "Aren't you ever tempted to give up?"

Andi and I look at each other mutely and then shake our heads. It's more than finding out what the truth is when it comes to situations like this. It's our excuse to spend weekends together while doing something cool and interesting.

"Not a chance," Andi adds, which leaves me feeling much warmer on this cold night.

After their odd little interview of us, we have supper together—and I have to admit, I'm impressed. I didn't hear the small army of cooks and servers it must have taken to put this feast together, but there is enough food to feed half the town. There's goose and game fowl, a slab of boar, venison, nut pies, and eggnog with enough booze in it to make my head spin a little.

"This is amazing," Andi breathes. I nod, my mouth already

full of goose and stuffing mere seconds after it hit my plate. There are only two servants: both slim, aging fellows, silent, with pointed beards and long noses. Dressed in green with white piping, they retrieve plates and fill dishes on request and then go back to their posts by the fireplace.

"It's a lot for just two guests." I'm wondering if Whitman's trying to dazzle us, or if this is just how he rolls.

"Oh, it's not just for the two of you—we'll have friends dropping by all night. I hold a feast for a full fortnight surrounding Christmas and New Year's." He winks, and I realize in the process of swallowing that he just handed us a clue.

"What happens when the last day of feasting ends?" Andi asks, picking up immediately on the slip. *Or is it only one?* If there's one thing I can tell, it's that Whitman has been in control of this interaction from the moment we walked in.

"Oh, the usual things one does once the holidays have fizzled out until Valentine's. Gather my decorations back up and bundle them into the attic for another year. Fortunately, I have some help. I couldn't do it all on my own at my age." He and Jack exchange a conspiratorial look...and I'm really left wondering.

Damn it, they only started giving up details about themselves once we got to the table. Should I just record them secretly? I know it's the only way I'll get any kind of record of the interview, but it seems rude.

Surreptitiously, I reach down into my pocket and poke the recorder switch. Maybe it's a little dirty—and I'm praying I hit the right button. But the Whitmans started playing dirty when they turned our our pre-dinner interview into ten minutes of introductions and getting-to-know-yous with Andi and I the only ones in the spotlight.

So far, all I have been able to do is verify a few things that strengthen our case for the Doc being involved in the mistletoe incident. He's the big Christmas fan, he and his son are wealthy, well connected and secretive, and he's been celebrating for the whole two weeks that the mistletoe has been up. But nothing he says gives a clue as to how he's doing it.

"Do you think that the mistletoe will go away once you stop your nightly celebrations?" I cut in. Andi looks up at me in mild confusion, but then nods. It's a little shady, but direct questions are getting us nowhere.

"Well, if the people responsible for decking the town have any respect for tradition, it won't stay up after dawn on the sixth." His eyes twinkle. It's the closest he's come after several tries, to admitting outright that he's the one behind all of this.

Andi and I exchange excited looks. It took me two hours this afternoon to put up the deer cams around town while she tried again to nap. They're on continuous record after dark for the next two days.

If something happens tomorrow night, we're going to catch it.

"You have said that you have nothing to do with this incident, Dr. Whitman, but there are indications that you might not be telling the whole truth." I offer a polite smile; the one he returns to me is tinged with mischief.

I keep my tone calmly earnest. "But let's work around that. Instead of asking how *you* did this, I'll just ask if you have any idea how it was done."

Jack lets out a soft laugh and elbows his father gently. Whitman chuckles again, appearing amused by the way I hedged around the question.

I keep my head up and watch him across the table. *Please let this thing be recording the conversation properly.*

The Doc considers his answer as the moments crawl past. Andi's hand finds mine under the table, and we clasp them tightly in mutual support.

"Well, from what you have told me, there was no sign of a

group large enough to get the job done moving around before dawn on the twenty-third of December. Nor were there any footprints left behind. Nor have footprints been left behind on new snow when a sprig is replaced. It is intriguingly odd." He tugs on his beard thoughtfully.

"Yes, Dr. Whitman, but how could it possibly have been done if no one was walking on the ground?" Andi's voice is almost pleading now. "And please don't say flying reindeer."

"No, no, no, of course not," Jack chimes in. "You would have seen the hoof-prints. Unless you didn't actually examine the rooftops for them?" Jack is really not helping right now. I shoot him a look, and he just grins with feigned innocence.

"Nothing so fancy, I suspect," Dr. Whitman says musingly. "You can cover snow tracks with a broom, after all, especially when there are layers of fallen snow and blowing wind to help you out. Also, footprints would not be needed or a ladder for the tall eaves, if someone drove past with people standing in the bed of a truck." The doctor's smile is infuriating. "It might be implausible, but it's not impossible."

I sit back. I know what he's hinting at, and the disappointment on Andi's face angers me a little. "Maybe. But that's a pretty hard sell. This mistletoe appeared inside a locked church and high above its doors and eaves—and it's all throughout the graveyard, so there was no driving a truck through."

"Seems to me a church would be immune to magic, being on sacred ground and all," Jack points out.

"Maybe Saint Nicholas gets a pass. He and the priest have the same boss, after all." Andi looks at him challengingly.

The Doc and his son both let out peals of laughter, the elder's loud and booming, filling the room. Even the servants titter a little. "Well said! Well said!" Jack snickers as he looks between the two of us. "Well, I can't say that you don't do your homework on these things."

Andi smiles with something like relief, and I clear my throat. "Anyway. None of the scenarios we have come up with get us any closer to sorting out a mundane way that all of this could have been coordinated and carried out in secret. Even if you're not responsible, you're the local Christmas expert. You must know something."

"I know some things, and perhaps you're right," Whitman concedes. "Perhaps something supernatural did occur." He takes a swallow of his hot spiced wine and then gestures with his mug. "The problem is that in the end, you're never going to find anything that reveals the whole truth behind this in a way that can be scientifically proven. Not even with all of your tech or all the scientists on your payroll back home."

"But why?" Andi asks softly. I hate the disappointed note in her voice.

"Because people won't believe," Jack cuts in. "Even when someone tells you exactly who they are and why they do what they do, you have trouble believing yourself."

I look down. I can't see if the recorder's going, but I speak as if it is. "Debunkers pit science against finding a wider view of reality, instead of aiding in the search for it. I'm trying to do the opposite."

The Doc shakes his head sadly. "But science isn't advanced enough yet. Humanity may not be either."

This is simultaneously the deepest and the craziest conversation I have ever been in. Please let this thing be recording!

"Anyway, you'll certainly get an interesting book out of your trip, and hopefully you'll get some new ideas. And even if you don't quite get what you want with that, you'll find that your greater aims here have been fulfilled. It was never entirely about the investigation, now was it?"

What the hell? Andi and I exchange glances, and I cough politely. "That's not actually accurate, Doc."

"Oh, it's perfectly accurate. If the two of you didn't chase the paranormal, you would find something else and pursue it with just as much passion. It could be rock climbing, bird photography, amateur archeology, or community theater."

He looks so smug that it pisses me off, but what he says next takes all the wind from my sails at once.

"What makes it special for the two of you is that you are doing it together."

I look at Andi, who's staring between the two of us in amazement, her cheeks so pink that I'd feel sorry for her if I wasn't so stunned. I always knew the exact reason why I've stayed in the business of paranormal investigations...and it looks like the last of Andi's denial just got burned away. "Oh," she mumbles.

I can see his beard twitching slightly as he tries to hide his amusement within it. "Oh, chin up, young lady, that doesn't mean that you won't have any success. It just means that if either one of you left your partnership, the other would not continue with this work."

He winks. "Tell me I'm wrong."

I can feel my ears prickling. But I can't say honestly that Whitman is wrong. I just can't understand his interest in us or his motive for constantly bringing the topic back to us and our relationship, no matter how hard we try to keep things focused.

Maybe he sees a lot more than I thought.

"Nobody said you were." I don't know how I'm keeping my voice quite so calm. "But that's not why we're doing this interview."

"Yes, I understand." he takes a few more bites from his plate, his face thoughtful, taking his time. "Of course it isn't."

"I think that what my dear old dad is trying to say is," Jack breaks with surprising gentleness, "some things in life are more important than trying to scientifically prove what is currently unprovable. And I'm with him in the belief that your time is best spent with each other, regardless of how you choose to spend it."

We answer with awkward smiles. The conversation turns towards some old stories of our adventures together, which we struggle through. My heart's pounding, and from the look on her face, Andi has been affected just as strongly.

I don't regret it afterward. My partner, on the other hand...

"I can't believe those people," Andi mutters as we drive back down the mountain. "I was looking for an interview on the Whitmans' involvement in this prank, and instead we spent more time talking to them about our relationship than anything else!"

I don't answer right away. It is very dark, even with the snowdrifts reflecting my headlights, and I drive carefully, wary of picking up too much speed on the slippery road. Worse, it looks like there's another snowstorm threatening. The sky between the bare trees is a starless, charcoal-colored haze.

"So the old guy's a hopeless romantic. Nobody loves Christmas that much and isn't a romantic." I hear that silence start to stretch out and let out a hard huff of air. "Andi. It's not perfect, and it was awkward, but we did get some quotes from him that will go well with it all."

There's so much more than that. I can feel the understanding growing between us now, the realization that we have too much unfinished business. Maybe I'm about to get that second chance I've always longed for.

If that's the case, I swear I'm not letting things fall apart again.

"Yeah, it's just..." She goes quiet as I slow down for a steep curve. "It feels like he's been teasing us this entire time."

"Teasing us? Or making it clear that some things are none of our business?" I keep my voice kind. I can tell she's totally exhausted.

"But why did he have to invade our privacy like that?" She frets slightly.

"Why not? We were trying our best to invade his. Hopeless romantic or not, he also wanted to discourage us from putting our noses in too deep."

She flops back against her seat in exasperation. "But why? Would it be so bad for humanity to know conclusively that some sweet, romantic display of magic is actually real?"

I couldn't accuse the mysterious pair of being malicious or selfish. So what could it be? "Maybe if people know too much about how he does this stuff, they'll try to stop him?"

Her eyes go slightly wide. "Do you think that's it? He's afraid he'll get the wrong kind of attention?"

"And they'll disrupt what he's doing." We turn onto the road leading into town over one of the two bridges that bracket it. "That makes as much sense as anything else I can come up with."

"That leaves me wondering how we handle this responsibly. This isn't the kind of event we want to discourage—especially in a place like New York." She relaxes, seeming very comforted by the idea that there's a good reason behind the Whitmans' evasiveness.

"Yeah, around here, folks need all the Christmas magic they can find. Life is tough, and the weather's brutal." I drive us into town as the first flakes start to fall. "Ugh, here we go again. Glad we left when we did."

"Yeah." She rubs her face and then glances at me as I stop to let a snowplow past on the cross street. "Do you think we should take the deer cams down, then?"

I frown. "Come on, sweetheart, you're the big believer. Even if we could have just as much fun hiking or spelunking or something, it doesn't mean you should give this up. You do love this stuff. We'll just have to figure out how to use what we find out tomorrow night."

She turns a game smile to me and nods, sighing. "I know you're right. I do. But it gets really, really tough to keep believing."

For a moment, her tone reminds me of earlier when she talked about needing to protect herself—from disappointment, from humiliation, from loss. Just like in love.

I put a hand on her shoulder. "You have more than enough proof to keep believing, sweetheart. At this point, we both do. You might not have enough proof for anyone else, but at least you and I are on the same page. Whatever this is, it is real, and it is very special."

That makes her smile as she gazes at me. "Well, you're definitely right about that."

9
ANDI

"Let's just check the audio and video in the morning," David yawns as we lug our stuff up the stairs. "I'm thinking cocoa and bed."

"I'm thinking cocoa and bed, too," I say thoughtfully as the biting cold wears off. I'm not sure we're quite on the same page as far as 'bed' goes, though. And I need to fix that now.

I know now that 'bed' was where I fell short in our relationship He never got good at giving me what I needed...but I never got good at asking.

We heat the leftover cocoa in the electric kettle while we peel off our outerwear and boots. The cold has deepened outside, but for some reason the walk back from the parking lot didn't leave me chilled the same way it did this morning. I'm fine.

I'm also on a mission.

"I hate to say it, but inappropriate as it was, the Doc had a serious point or two." My socks are actually sweaty from being in the heavy boots and socks. *How did I nearly freeze earlier?*

I'm getting used to the idea that I may never know, but it's a bitter pill. So it's better to think about other things. Much more pleasant things.

"About us?" Poor David sounds so hopeful that I have to bite back a laugh.

"Yeah, us and ghost hunting. I love the chase, David, I do, but I wouldn't bother with it if I wasn't doing it with you." It takes all my courage to look him in the eyes and admit that, but it's time.

He stares at me as my heart thunders, and then he drops his boots with a clunk. Outside, the wind rises to a wail, shaking the windows slightly, but I barely notice. For a brief moment, the sound nags at me slightly—like there's something I'm forgetting.

Then I'm in his arms again, and I forget everything but his kiss.

The first times we ever kissed were pure magic, even if they were clumsy with enthusiasm. It's like that now—except for the way he slides his fingers up the back of my skull to grasp my hair firmly by the roots. I whimper, shocked and excited; he teases at my tongue with his until I slowly start to respond. His other arm is around my waist, holding me firmly as I slide my hands up his chest.

I hold him so tightly, like I'll never let him go. He's still a big kid in some ways, but not in the ways that used to drive me crazy. I'm tired of stopping myself from trying again by telling myself that people don't change. He has.

It just took a holiday miracle and a life-threatening crisis to really show me how much.

Seducing him took less work than I thought it would. But finally, we both run out of breath, and he breaks the kiss and backs off slightly, looking down at me as we pant mutely.

"You have no idea how glad I am to hear you say that," he mutters huskily, his breath blowing warm air on my tingling lips.

The old anger and frustration that soured me on sex with him have lost so much of their strength that I can barely feel them. "It's become pretty damn clear we'd better...work this out," I murmur against his lips a moment before he kisses me again.

It's rougher this time, and I return the favor, digging my fingertips into the muscle of his shoulders and pressing against him eagerly. But after several delicious moments, he backs off again, looking cautiously down at me.

"I'm getting horny as hell here, sweetheart. If you want me to go, tell me now." I can feel the tremor in his body, and he's sipping air like he can't get it all the way down into his lungs. Back in the day, he would have already been taking off my clothes without seeing if I was into it. Now, he restrains himself.

Intriguing.

I look up at him and then deliberately slide my hand down to cup the crotch of his pants, feeling the fabric straining to contain his cock. He groans through his teeth and looks down at me with an anguished expression. "I want you to stay," I tell him firmly.

This time when he kisses me he lifts me as well—no small feat, since I'm no small woman. Startled, I throw my arms around his neck and let out a sharp whimper against his mouth.

He carries me to the bed and I flash back to this morning, when I was too distracted by cold to notice that he did the same then. Before he used his body to warm me without making a single move outside of a sleepy kiss.

It's *very* promising. After all, too much impatience is the death of good sex.

As soon as he settles me on the bed I start tearing off my clothes impatiently. He stares for a moment as I struggle out of way too many layers—then he eagerly starts stripping down as well.

David called me an Amazon once, and I'd never forgotten that comment—but as he stares down at me hungrily the last of my self-consciousness starts to dissolve. He likes my tall body with its bountiful curves, its firm, heavy breasts and powerful thighs. He's seen it before; the touch of his gaze doesn't make me uncomfortable.

Anything but. His worshipful look as he takes me in from head to toe before pulling off his long johns makes me feel like a goddess.

He really has filled out nicely under those woolens—his body still lean but well-muscled, his treasure trail a little thicker but his belly just as flat. I run my hands over him, brushing my hand briefly over his thick, well-groomed cock, which is as silky smooth as I remember.

The wind screams outside the windows and the lights flicker as he joins me in bed. Again, I feel like I'm forgetting something. But this is more important. I push it to the back of my head and wrap my arms around him.

For just a moment I tense up, because when I embrace him, I wonder if he'll pull the same uncomfortable trick he used to and push his way inside me before I'm quite ready. But he holds back instead, his hands running over me almost too slowly as he explores my body in a new way.

He has a strangely serious look on his face as he caresses me, his hands warm and firm on my skin. I can feel his cock brushing against my thigh. My eyes close, and I let myself relax under his hands while he keeps up his caresses, taking his time.

Every time he finds a spot that makes me gasp, he strokes me there again and again until I'm shaking. My nape, my collarbones, the spot just under my breasts, my hips, and the tops of my thighs all get as much attention as my tits and bountiful ass, which he's always been obsessed with. "Like that?" he purrs in my ear as he runs two fingers around my nipple and then rolls it gently between them.

I arch slightly and nod, making a small sound of pleasure.

He grins and slides down my body, starting to kiss my neck as his hands knead and stroke my breasts.

I stretch under him, enjoying his weight over me again now that he's not trying to rush the encounter. In fact, his teasing is starting to get me very, very turned on.

He's found the spots that make me moan and goes after them feverishly, his hands firm and sure. Crouched over my thighs on his powerful knees, he kneads my ass roughly with his hands as his mouth takes over their work. I tremble and moan as he covers me with slow kisses...and then I thrash suddenly, overloaded by unfamiliar pleasure.

He pauses with his lips inches from my breast and looks up at me. My heart is beating too hard and my body is too tense; the intensity of sensation almost hurts. Propping himself up, he purrs, "Roll over."

Moments later, he has me on my side with him snugged up behind me, cock sliding over the small of my back as he kisses and nips at my neck and shoulders. His hands knead my breasts, stroking their thumbs back and forth over my nipples while I squirm and gasp.

I can feel him shuddering with need behind me, his cock throbbing hard against my skin. But still, he takes his time. His hands and mouth slowly move down my body, leaving a trail of stinging love-bites down my spine while his fingers move to dig gently into the hollows of my hipbones.

I rub my ass back against him, and he growls and squeezes the twin globes roughly. My cunt aches for him in a way I can't remember feeling since I was sixteen and didn't even know what sex was like. Now, unexpectedly, I'm learning what it *can* be like.

"Can you roll back over for me, sweetheart?" he breathes in my ear after a while, and I know what he's after. I want it, too—his mouth on my breasts, his body on mine. But then...I hesitate.

My mind fills with images from the amazingly sexy dreams

I've been having, and I smile, suddenly inspired. "I have a better idea."

"Holy shit," David groans as he settles back against a pile of pillows I've heaped on the bedstead. His cock is so hard that it gleams. He looks up at me in amazement as I kneel over him, positioning myself.

"Don't you dare bust yet," I warn him, and he grins and nods, a little wide-eyed. I take hold of his cock, and he grunts as his head rolls back, fingers digging into the bedding. I fit him between my now-slick folds and start to lower myself.

"Aaaah!" he gasps, body straining under me suddenly, eyes flying open. He pants hoarsely as he struggles to keep it together; I slide further and further down, feeling him stretch me open inside. Finally, I settle over him completely, my knees sinking into the pillows as he moans low in his throat.

I hold still; we hold each other until his tremors relax, and he starts to caress me again.

I don't know why he's so confident until he takes hold of the small of my back with one hand and bends me back a little, nuzzling my breasts. His other hand settles between us...and takes hold of my labia right over my clit. His thumb dips into the warm slit there...and starts to circle delicately, then more firmly.

I moan softly and start to squirm, feeling the ache inside me bloom into growing pleasure. Every swipe of his thumb, every stroke of his fingers, leaves me trembling and clenching on him just a little bit harder.

"Oh," I whimper before I can stop myself, and I start squirming, rocking my hips slightly against him. He groans but lifts his hips gently, letting me set the pace. He's cheating, though; his stroking hand drives me to move more and more vigorously.

It feels so good that it almost hurts. My cunt tightens around him even more, and I feel my juices making him slick and easier to ride. My head falls back—and then I let out a sharp cry as his mouth closes on my nipple.

He starts to lap at me in time with his strokes, making me ride him harder as my hips roll reflexively. He grunts against my skin and lashes his tongue harder, while his hand keeps moving against my wet, sensitive flesh until my breath burns in my lungs.

I'm riding him rough now, grinding wildly, trembling harder and harder while he starts to shake as well. I can hear my voice rising in sharp cries as I hang onto him for dear life. Stunned, a little scared, but greedy for sensation, I press my cunt against his hand and then rock against him harder as he speeds his caresses.

I don't know what's happening. It's too much. It's almost terrifying. I open my mouth to tell him to stop—but what comes out is, "Oh, God, *yes*—"

My muscles seize up as my voice rises into a wail. I thrash over him, exploding with sudden energy as the pleasure ramps up into ecstasy.

I sob with joy, my body going rigid with each contraction, and swooning and trembling in between. As everything comes apart, I hear him groan hoarsely against my skin, and I grind on him more, so that the groan becomes a long shout. Then his cock lets loose in several long shudders, and his hips almost lift me off the bed before he collapses.

The pleasure shocked me, and now I'm shocked by my sudden exhaustion, even as I feel ready to float away on a cloud of bliss. I sway over him, chest heaving for air.

Somehow, he manages to catch me before I can collapse, and I slide down limply as I lay down over him. My knees pop as I dismount from him; I'm speechless, tingling, barely noticing the brief pain.

"Do you like that, sweetheart?" he purrs in my ear as I lie trembling on his chest.

"Uh huh," I manage to mumble, and he laughs.

"Good."

It's David's laugh that wakes me hours later, well after dawn. I sit up, sleepy and confused, and see him standing half-dressed, long johns still unbuttoned and loose around him as he faces the window—a window that is covered in streaky ice.

"You've got to be kidding me," he snorts as I blink past him at the icy view. "A fucking ice storm on top of everything?"

I grab my robe and pull it on, moving to his side. My legs are wobbly and a little sore, but I'm so relaxed that I barely care. I've never felt better about rethinking my stance on anything in my life.

"Ice storm?" I fish my phone out of my jacket pocket and check the weather report. "Not much of one. It moved on hours ago. They should have the roads cleared and in good condition again before lunch."

"Well, that's good, at least," he sighs. "But there's just one problem."

A shock goes through me. "The deer cams!"

We manage to do the smart thing and bundle up before we go to check the six cameras that have put up around town. We walk out to check them arm in arm, as much to help me keep my balance on the icy sidewalk as anything. People are already wandering the streets on their morning errands, but the crowds are thinner.

"Think the tourists are hiding inside until they salt the sidewalks?" I ask as we move toward the first camera site.

"Probably a good bet." We reach the first shop that let us install a camera under their eaves, and he grabs his penlight to check it. "Well, this one's intact, but the light's off. Cold may have drained the battery."

He takes it down—and we both gape in shock as he opens the battery casing to find it full of ice crystals. "Or killed the battery for good. Holy shit."

"Let's check the others." I'm really starting to worry now... though the fear has no real teeth to it any more. That might have something to do with the company, though.

My worries are well-founded, as it turns out. The second shop had a leak in its awning that we didn't notice, and we find the camera literally frozen inside a large icicle. Two more cameras broke loose in the high wind—we find them broken, lenses and casings shattered. The rest have battery problems like the first.

"Well, looks like the mistletoe will be down tomorrow with no magic involved at all," David sighs as he looks around, fists on hips. The bag of broken cameras hangs from his side; he doesn't seem bothered by this last setback. Good sex can do that, and so can a change in perspective.

We've had both.

"You're right. Warm front's moving in. It will rise above freezing tomorrow. They'll all just fall off on their own."

"And this time no one will replace them." He wraps his arms around me, sighing. "Look, we're done here. Let's go home? I have an unopened bottle of New Year's champagne with our names on it."

I look around again, a sad, wistful feeling in my heart, like that of a kid at bedtime on Christmas night. "There's always next year," I say, half to myself. Then I look up at him and hug him back briefly. "Let's go."

10

DAVID

As it turned out, the last interview didn't record. Our enlightening dinner conversation with the Whitmans had been meant for our eyes—and ears—only. For all my usual careful attention to detail, I had somehow forgotten to charge the audio recorder's built-in battery.

Instead, we've got a lovely video of Andi and I talking about how we fell in love and how much we enjoy our work together, surreptitiously shot by that sneaky bastard Jack and left for me like a gift. I think I owe him some champagne.

It took us only a month to put the book together. It's being edited now with several breathtaking shots of the town and the mountains around it being worked in. The one thing we were able to do, besides talk to people and record a few interviews, was take a lot of pictures.

But the video—the interview, the attempts to interview Jack, all that stuff either just leads to more questions and greater mysteries or exposes personal revelations about us—although I've edited it together nicely, I still don't know whether we should release it on our website.

It's not just that parts of it are very personal. I have no

problem shouting to the fucking hills that I got my second chance and that the two of us are going strong as lovers and work partners both. I naturally want to check with Andi first, but that's not the only thing restraining me.

It's the rest of it. The baffled but amused residents, the retired movie star with his new lover and tiny child, the huffy priest's daughter and her enormous biker boyfriend, laughing Jack saying he's Jack Frost himself…it's all personal and weird as hell. How much of it will appeal to the public at large?

More importantly, how much of it is right to release?

I sit back from my computer, rolling my stiff shoulders and standing up to walk out of my office. My penthouse is arranged around a central atrium with a hothouse inside; beyond its glass walls, I can see the bed where Andi is still curled up, sleeping.

I exhausted her again. The thought still makes me proud. Amazing what a little effort, patience, and communication can do.

I move over to one of my enormous, insulated-glass windows, this one overlooking the fenced deck with its covered outdoor pool and jacuzzi. Beyond it, the city sits frozen in the grip of winter, millions of lights gleaming in the icy dark. I tighten my smoking jacket closer around me and go to pour myself a brandy before returning to my desk.

I play part of Jack's interview again. *"My name's Jack Frost as I told you before. I'm ageless, I live at the North Pole with my father Saint Nicholas, and my job is bringing the fall colors and the winter frosts."*

"Damn it, that sounds like satire," I grumble under my breath, sitting back in my chair. *No superhuman being would actually walk up to us and introduce himself like that. And even if he did, no one would ever believe it.*

Which means that we can't use the interview. It will kill any credibility this investigation has.

I rub my face in exasperation. "You did that on purpose, didn't you, Jack?" I can't really hate him anymore though, even if this shit frustrates me. He did help Andi and I get back together—even if he did it with a stolen kiss.

A flash of movement on the balcony catches my attention. I could have sworn I saw a man-sized figure in a dark coat. But when I look again, there's no one there.

There's something I didn't notice before, hanging from the eaves. And a mark on the glass.

I stare. Then I grab my camera—after checking the battery—and quickly take a few photos. I'm smiling like crazy. We probably can't use these either—except for ourselves.

She's still going to love them.

I look back once more as I quit my computer and get up to head back to bed. They're still there: my evidence, real evidence, and something like an answer. Even if no one would ever believe us.

A curlicue of frost shaped like a fern frond on the insulated window...and a frozen, dried bit of mistletoe fastened to our balcony overhang sixteen stories above the ground.

The End.

SIGN UP TO RECEIVE FREE BOOKS

Sign Up to Receive Free E-Books and Audiobook Codes.

Would you like to read **The Unexpected Nanny, Dirty Little Virgin** and **other romance books** for **free**?

You can sign up to receive these free e-books and audiobooks by typing this link into your browser:

https://www.steamyromance.info/free-books-and-audiobooks-hot-and-steamy/

Or this one:

https://www.steamyromance.info/the-unexpected-nanny-free/

PREVIEW OF HIS HIDDEN LOVE
A REVERSE HAREM ROMANCE THEIR SECRET DESIRE BOOK 1

By Megan Lee
Ivy Wonders

Blurb

India Blue is one of the world's most successful and beloved singers. The beautiful Seattle native fiercely guards her privacy and for good reason—when she was a teenager, a horrific attack changed her forever. Since that day, she has avoided intimacy, excepting only Sun, the gorgeous Korean pop star, India's friend and sometime lover, who would change his life for her—even going so far as leaving his true love, bandmate Tae.

When India meets superstar actor Massimo Verdi, she is thrown into a world of passion, desire, and uninhibited sensuality. India knows she is falling for the charming, sexy Italian. When he seemingly betrays that trust, India wonders if either of her lovers is the man for her or is she merely a consolation prize?

Still violently obsessed with India, her attacker will soon be released from prison. To be safe, India must disappear into obscurity, but she cannot bring herself to part from either Massimo or Sun.

But are Sun or Massimo the men she believes them to be? Or will her heart lead her to a darker, more treacherous place than she could have imagined?

Secret Love Song is the first part in a series of connected stories with an international cast of beautiful people, stunning locations, dark storylines, and hot, hot sensual romance with no cheating and a guaranteed happy ever after!

When singer India Blue meets superstar actor Massimo Verdi, their sexual attraction is immediate and almost overwhelming. But India is plagued by a dark secret, and when her life is threatened, the two would-be-lovers find their love inundated with jeopardy and distance.

Complicating matters is India's close relationship with her friend, K-pop star Sun, who is in turmoil as well. After photographs of Massimo kissing his ex-girlfriend flood the internet, India flees to Seoul where she and the distressed Sun rekindle their sexual relationship.

With two men in her heart and another determined to kill her, India becomes mired in uncertainty and depression. When she and Massimo reconnect, she begins to see a way of out of her gloom and falls in love with him...

...except her vengeful psychopath is never far behind. With more secrets getting revealed, India needs to decide who to love —and who to trust.

Massimo Verdi, international playboy and one of the world's sexiest actors, is still single after ending a decade-long romance when he meets American singer India Blue and is instantly bowled over by her.

Frustrated by India's apparent flightiness, Massimo tries to forget her and gets caught up in a scandal involving his manipulative ex-girlfriend, Valentina.

After photos of them kissing are published, Massimo thinks he has lost India forever but when she reaches out to him, their friendship blossoms and soon becomes romantic in nature.

As much as he is falling for her, Massimo can see that India's life is convoluted, and he fears that could lose the woman he loves to a deranged stalker.

Can he risk his heart? What about India's secret past and her love for another man in another country? Can Massimo trust her to love him alone or will he need to put his ego aside to capture the heart of the most incredible woman he has ever met?

CHAPTER ONE - WICKED GAME

Venice, Italy

India Blue inhaled as much oxygen as she could through her nose, then let it out slowly through her mouth. The breath juddered from her in a shaky, almost gasp-like hiss. It was always this way: the nerves before the concert started, the heinous half-hour of self-doubt. Her stage fright was well documented and that gave her a measure of comfort. The people who paid to hear her sing knew she got panicky; if they were a decent crowd, they'd give her that bit extra to get her adrenaline flowing.

At least that's what she hoped—that they'd be kind. Even after all this time, she had trouble believing in the screams and the joy she received when she waved to the thousands of fans that filled her concerts. She had felt like an awkward, bashful teenager when all of this started—when she was able to function once more after the incident.

God. Why are you thinking of this now?

India tasted bile and was about to dissolve into a full-blown panic attack. Not a good situation when she was due on stage in five minutes. She pulled her long dark hair back into a messy ponytail—no stylists or makeup for her—she preferred the intimacy of making herself up, of getting her hair just the way she wanted. She never was a fashionista despite the high-end designers scrambling to sign the beautiful, young Indian-American girl. India checked her reflection: huge dark-brown eyes, pink mouth, golden skin. People considered her beautiful but the haunted look in her eyes never went away, and that was *all* she could see in her reflection.

India grabbed her phone to check the time. Four minutes to curtain up. Being allowed to play at La Fenice, Venice's premier opera house, was a testament to her talent. So far, she was one of a handful of non-classical artists to do so. Her signature mix of pop, country, and jazz was unique, certainly, but she never liked being confined by genres.

"Hey, Bubba."

As soon as India heard her brother's voice, all her tension drained. Technically, Lazlo Schuler was not a blood relative but he was the one she trusted the most—and there weren't many.

"Hey bro. Just about to go on."

Lazlo gave a deep chuckle. "I wish I could be there to see you, Bubba. This is a special night."

India sighed. "It's okay, Laz, I understand what you have to deal with over there."

"How come you're my only client who I never have trouble with?" Lazlo laughed. He was her manager, her publicist, her everything, but he also had other clients on his roster—clients who demanded his attention day and night. At forty-nine, Lazlo was resolutely single, married to his job and the best in the business. "You heard from Gabe, Bubba?" Lazlo's brother worked in Los Angeles.

"A text message. He and Selena are really splitting up, huh?"

Lazlo sighed. "At this point, it's probably the best for both.

Flogging a dead horse and all that. Listen, I hate to be a nag but by my watch, you should have been on stage a minute ago."

India glanced at the clock. "Shit. Look, thanks, Laz, I'll call you later."

"Love you, Bubba. Hey, say hello to Diana and Grey."

India grinned. "Will do. Love you, bro."

As she walked to the stage, less anxious now that she had spoken to Lazlo, she thought about her plans after the show. She was having a late dinner and drinks with her best friends, Diana Harper and Grey Lynch, a married couple, two English actors she had been close friends with for years now. Back in the day, India scored a film of Diana's, when she herself was a music star, and they'd been friends ever since. Diana was flirty, feisty, and fun; twenty-two years senior to India's twenty-eight, and India considered her a sister. Diana had counseled her through some hard times, and her husband Grey, a laidback sweetheart, had become a close friend as well.

Later this evening, she would meet with them and their friend, Massimo. India's heart began to beat a little faster. Massimo Verdi was Italy's biggest movie star: attractive, dark-brown curls, intense green eyes, a body to die for, and a rich, masculine voice that sent chills through her. She'd never met him; Diana was close friends with him and he asked to meet her, much to India's surprise. Her first instinct was to say no; the crushing weight of her tragic history stifling her. Diana had seen her discomfort and firmly sat her down.

"Sweetheart...it's *just* dinner. Massimo's a sweetie...once you get past the machismo and that marvelous face of his. He's a fan and wants to meet you. And for whatever it's worth...I think you'll like him."

So, she agreed, much to Diana's delight. A few evenings ago, she was in Rome, and Diana made them watch one of Massimo's movies. Diana was right, he is *divine*. The role he played was a tortured artist, manipulated by the woman he loved. He was hypnotic in the role, and she could not stop thinking about him ever since.

"Hey, India, you ready? They're foaming at the mouth for you."

India smiled at the stagehand, pushed her thoughts of Massimo Verdi to the back of her mind, and stepped out on the stage.

Massimo hugged Diana and Grey hello, and they walked directly to their private box to watch the show. The lights were already down as they took their seats, and the first swirling notes of music commenced. Massimo smiled at Diana.

"I've been looking forward to this day."

Diana grinned back. "Good! You know, right about now, India will be at the side of the stage trying not to vomit."

Massimo laughed. "I understand that emotion."

Diana rolled her eyes. "*Sure* you do."

Massimo smirked and shrugged. His face, his body, his voice had power. His confidence was well-earned, and he often concealed how shy he really was.

The music got louder and the screams and applause of the fans went into overdrive as India Blue stepped into the spotlight. The roar of the audience along with the sight of her in the flesh for the first time, lit dramatically by concert lights, sent adrenaline shooting through his veins and he leaned eagerly forward.

The first note she sung made him shiver. So pure and clear, then as the song continued, her legendary rasp came in—so much emotion, so much honesty. Massimo was enraptured. She was petite but leggy with breakneck curves and a small waist, and the way her dark hair was escaping from the bun on the back of her neck made him crazy. He could feel his groin tighten as he watched her move. She was not a singer with highly stylized shows, backup dancers, or intricate, well-practiced dance moves. Instead, she swayed with the rhythm when she was at the mic or sitting at her piano, her whole body seeming to merge with the instrument. It was not sexual, nor her writhing meant to titillate. India Blue was an individual so connected with her music that everything she had went into the performance.

To Massimo, it was the singularly most erotic thing he'd seen and he knew, without doubt, that he wanted India Blue in his bed and in his life.

India high-fived every member of her band making sure they got equal applause. It was one of the reasons session musicians clamored to work with her: she paid well over-standard rates; she was inclusive; collaborative; and best of all, she loved. She treated them as family and never put herself above them, even though it was her name on the marquee bringing the audiences —and the money—rolling in.

As she began the encore, she glanced up to the box where she knew Diana, Grey, and Massimo Verdi were sitting. She smiled and waved at them who smiled back, and then she looked at *Massimo*. He was staring at her, his eyes intense, and she could not tear her own eyes away from him. At the first line of the song—a slow, sensual cover of Chris Isaak's "Wicked Game"—suddenly only the two of them were in the room.

The world was on fire and all that could save me was you...
India never sung a more honest line.

CHAPTER TWO - I'LL BE SEEING YOU

India showered quickly, her heart thumping. In a few moments, she would be meeting the man who she sang a freaking *love song* to in front of thousands of people.

What were you thinking? She berated herself as she dried her hair, leaving it down so she could hide behind it. She slipped into a loose-fitting lilac swing dress that showed off her long legs and the cinnamon tone of her skin. A delicate long chain cuddled between her breasts, the lightest of makeup on her face. India glanced in the mirror. The haunted look was there. With it, something else. Something new. *Excitement.*

Before she decided to cancel, she grabbed her purse and went out to meet her friends—and the man who put that excitement in her.

Disappointment shot through her when Diana and Grey were alone. *You scared him off.* She swallowed the sting and happily greeted her friends. Diana beamed at her. "You were fantastic, darling, and utterly spellbinding." She lowered her voice to a stage-whisper. "You had quite the effect on our Italian friend."

India colored, and Grey shot his wife a warning glance

tempered with a smile. "Leave the poor girl alone. Sorry, sweetheart," Grey kissed India's cheek, "I married a pimp. Massi had to use the bathroom."

"And he's returned!" Diana crowed suddenly, and India's stomach twisted into knots when he spoke behind her.

"*Buona sera.*" His voice was even deeper in person, like dark chocolate. India turned to look at him, hoping the blatant lust she was feeling wasn't too obvious. He was tall, at least six-two, dwarfing her five-five. His eyes searched her face in a way that made her feel she was already naked and about to be fucked into next Tuesday by him. He *oozed* sex. There was a precarious intensity to him that made him look angry, menacing...and then he smiled.

Oh, dear God...that smile. His expression altered from manly to boyish in a split second—from dangerous to sweet. *Damn.* India was gaping at him and hoped she wasn't *actually* drooling. She tentatively smiled back at him. "Hey there. Great to meet you at last."

Massimo Verdi leaned in and kissed her cheek, only lingering for a second longer. His scent was woodsy and clean, a tiny hint of expensive tobacco underneath. His mouth was perfectly shaped and soft against her cheek.

India took a breath to compose herself, glancing over to Diana and Grey who were talking amongst themselves. There was a gleam in Diana's eyes when her friend returned her attention. "Shall we go and dine, loves? I'm starving."

Diana was an expert at 'innocent' manipulation, Massimo thought to himself with a smirk, as his friend deftly arranged them at table so he sat next to India. Not that he minded – India Blue was everything he'd imagined and so much more. The soft beauty of her features—those dark eyes and those lips—he was already having fantasies about that pink mouth of hers.

He noticed Diana slip India a phone under the table, and India, without looking, typed in something and handed it back. Massimo half-grinned when he caught India's eye. She subtly put a finger over her lips; it was obviously some kind of prank. He winked at her and gave the tiniest nod—*I got your back.*

As she sat next to him, he couldn't help but notice the bare skin of her thigh—such a glorious golden color. He wanted to run his hand along her smooth skin...

"Massi?"

Massimo tore his attention away from India's thigh. Diana was smiling at him. "Massi, we watched *Sole Scuro* the other night, and I have to tell you—sorry to rat you out, Indy—but by the end, Indy was screaming bloody murder at the television."

India and Grey laughed, and Massimo smiled, turning to the woman at his side. "You were?"

She nodded. "That guy was setting you up the entire time! I was livid!" Massimo was amused at her indignation.

"She kept yelling, '*No! Don't let him do that!*' Although the language was quite a bit coarser." Grey shook his head in mock-disappointment.

India leaned closer to Massimo. "I actually had to be reminded that it wasn't *real.*"

Massimo laughed. "Well, I hope not! I died at the end of that movie."

Diana cackled, and India burst out laughing. "You heartless *wench.*"

The men joined the laughter as Diana waved her hands. "No, I'm not happy about that, just at the memory of *somebody* getting a little teary." She looked pointedly at India who flushed scarlet and shot back.

"Yes. It was *Grey.*"

"Fibber." Diana rolled her eyes and smirked at Massimo.

Grey decided to help India out. "I have to say, it *was* sad."

"Yeah, see?" India looked so incensed that Massimo couldn't resist brushing the back of his hand against her cheek for the briefest second.

"I'm touched that you enjoyed it."

India gratefully smiled at him. "You were amazing, Massimo, in all seriousness. Spellbinding!"

Their eyes met and, for just that brief moment, their gaze locked. They were interrupted by the arrival of their food, but the ice had been broken. Massimo was indebted to Diana; the woman knew how to make any situation seem natural and so much fun. He smiled at her appreciatively; she looked back with a question in her eyes. *You like her?* He nodded; the slight movement to acknowledge that, yes, he did like this young woman sitting next to him.

All four chatted and laughed for the rest of the feast and then lingered over drinks. For Massimo, it was nice to relax with friends and not get harassed by the press. He easily engaged India in conversation, talking about how much he enjoyed her concert.

"Your voice is like liquid silk," he said thoughtfully, "but then there's the kick of deep claret in there, too. Like a hot chili in chocolate. Sensual, dark, affecting."

India was blushing and he loved the rose pink against her golden skin. "Thank you, that's a divine thing to say."

"I was telling Massimo about your music video project," Diana interjected, all innocence but her eyes twinkling. "Indy, wouldn't Massi be the *perfect* leading man for it?"

India's face went red, but she beamed and looked at Massimo. "You *would* be," her voice shook endearingly, "but I couldn't suppose…"

"I'd love to," he said, pushing away the thought his agent would kill him for agreeing to something without consulting her. But the hell with it—anything to spend more time with this lovely woman. "We should arrange a time to discuss it while you're in the country. How long will you be here for?"

She hesitated. "A while. I'm not certain on exact dates but at least a month."

Massimo relaxed. "Then we have all the time in the world." Again, their eyes locked and held, and if Diana and Grey hadn't been there, he would have leaned over and pressed his lips to hers...

Suddenly, tinny music erupted, and as Grey's phone belted out "I'm Too Sexy" loudly, he exclaimed "You little minx!" to India, who dissolved into giggles. "How the heck did you manage to change my ring tone...again? *Every* time!" He shook his head trying not to smile, and Massimo realized what Diana and India had been doing earlier. "She does this to me *every* time and I never catch her," Grey explained to Massimo, who started to laugh. Diana looked innocent, but India gleefully blew a kiss at Grey.

"I have my ways, Lynch. Magic sticky fingers."

"Magic *something*." Grey grumbled, then grinned at his young friend. "I suppose "I'm Too Sexy" is better than what you set it to last time." He adjusted his phone settings. "She changed it to "Ain't Nothin' like Gangbang," " he told Massimo who choked on his drink. "And my agent called me...in front of my *mother*."

India whooped and high-fived Diana and then gave Grey a cheesy sneer when he scowled at her in mock-disapproval. Massimo smiled. These were good people to be around: fun, no fake airs and graces. Their table attracted a lot of attention merely for who was sitting there but thankfully, they were left in peace to take pleasure in their evening.

"So, tell me," he asked India, who was still adorably flushed with victory from her prank, "This project....is it a music video?"

India nodded. "Actually, it's more of a short film, a story of a relationship in four songs. The theme is built around suspicion, heartbreak, separation, and tragedy. Not the most original, but I'm hoping the visuals and the music will provide the originality. I'd really like to film it here in Venice and use some masquerade visuals in it."

"Did you perform any of the songs tonight?"

India shook her head. "No, they're not quite ready…I have some clips on my phone. Would you like to hear them?"

For a world-famous music star, India Blue was not conceited in the slightest, Massimo thought, as he put in the ear buds she offered. She was nervous at allowing him to listen to the songs, her dark eyes curious and slightly fearful of his rejection.

As she pressed *play*, his ears were filled with her sweet, husky voice, and Massimo felt his whole body react to the sound. It was as if he could hear every ounce of heartbreak and pain she ever had… He closed his eyes for a moment, immersing himself in the sound, then as he looked back at her, he imagined her with her tears flowing down her cheeks as her lover left, as her heart was ripped from her. Massimo saw her darkness and knew…it wasn't just the music. *What happened to you?* The thought of anyone—a lover, an enemy—hurting her made him want to protect her. The song ended and slowly he removed the ear buds.

"Wow. Just wow." To his astonishment, his voice shook and he giggled.

"Can you find a character for that?" She said softly and without thinking, he cupped her face in his palms.

"I could—although I could kill him for hurting you." His thumb gently stroked across her cheek. He could feel her trembling.

Unexpectedly, they noticed Diana and Grey had left the table. India, checking her watch and seeing it was after midnight, frowned. "Where'd they go?"

Massimo hid a smile. "I think they are, how do you say, being...discreet."

His arm was along the back of her chair, his fingers stroking the inside of her arm. India looked at him, studying his face. "They are?"

Massimo nodded but remained silent. India's eyes registered desire—but also panic.

"So, this was...a plan?"

Massimo shook his head. "No, not a plan, I swear. I had no idea they would leave us alone. If you prefer, I can call you a cab. Are you uncomfortable, *Bella*?"

India shook her head. One beat of hesitation, then Massimo leaned in and lightly brushed his lips against hers. She tasted like red wine, and she responded softly to the kiss. He drew back, questioning. Her dark brown eyes were unreadable.

"*Scusami, signore? Signora?* Your companions asked me to send this over with this note." The waiter put down a bottle of champagne and handed India the note.

She opened and read it, starting to both laugh and blush furiously. Massimo was curious. "What does it say, *Bella*?"

India hesitated for a second and then handed it to him. As he read it, Massimo too began to laugh. "Well, now..."

The note read:

Dear Disgracefully Gorgeous People,
Thank you for a lovely evening. Now go! Get naked and fuck each other senseless because you've been practically doing that all evening. I say, Huzzah!
We love you both!
D & G xxx
PS
The check has been settled.

India and Massimo examined the note, then each other before bursting out laughing again. Massimo rose and offered India his hand. "How about a stroll through the city?"

India accepted his hand, feeling it close over hers, his fingers warm and dry. His thumb stroked the back of her hand as they walked. Every cell in her body was reacting to this man and without a shadow of a doubt, India knew that soon they would be in bed, fucking and clawing at each other like wild bunnies. It seemed inevitable. A frisson of electricity coursed over her skin at the thought.

So…she was amazing herself. She *never* did this: a one-night stand—to her, it just wasn't worth it. But she'd never been as turned on as she was right now. She wanted him inside her, wanted to kiss him, bite him, and suck him. She felt breathless with arousal and desire, and when a few streets later, he gently backed her against a wall and kissed her, she sank into it, her hands curling around his neck as his lips moved against hers. His fingers stroked her belly, sending thrills through her.

"God, you're beautiful," he whispered, and India sighed as his hand slipped under her skirt and began to caress her through her panties. Her hand snaked down to cup his rock-hard cock. God, he was *huge*. His eyes glittered with unreleased desire, and it took her breath away.

"My place is a couple of streets away." She gazed into his eyes. He nodded, his smile replaced by a torrid look of desire. *What a dangerous man,* she thought with a shiver. *What an exciting, irresistible man...*

Her cell phone rang, and she ignored it as Massimo kissed her again, his tongue slipping in and caressing hers. His eyelashes brushed her cheek as his arms tightened around her. Her cell phone squawked again, this time with the familiar '911' ringtone she reserved for emergencies.

She broke away from Massimo, out of breath and with an

apologetic smile. "I'm so sorry, I have to get that. It's my brother's emergency ring tone."

"You and your ring tones," he grinned, "I'll step over here for a moment."

He moved away to give her some privacy and for a moment India just watched him. He took out a cigarette and lit it, shooting her a smile. God, he was delicious. India smiled back and answered her phone.

"Seriously, Laz, this better be good. You have no idea what you're interrupting."

There was a silence on the other end of the phone, and India frowned. "Laz?"

"Bubba...I'm sorry...are you alone?"

"No, I'm with Massimo, a friend...what is it, Laz? What's wrong?"

"After I tell you this, can you ask this Massimo to escort you home? I don't want you alone."

India's body began to tremble. Lazlo was not a panicky guy, nor was he prone to dramatics. "Laz, you're scaring me."

"It's Carter, Bubba. The arresting officer was charged with corruption, and all of his cases have been thrown out. They let Carter out a week ago, and so far, he's in the wind. He's out. He got out of prison."

CHAPTER THREE - LET'S GET LOST

India's entire body went numb. "It can't be, Laz... How could they let him out? The evidence was overwhelming! I testified, for the love of God!" She became aware Massimo was listening, alarmed. She looked at him apologetically. He approached and put his arms around her. For a second, she resisted; she didn't want this crap to sully their evening, and he was still technically a stranger, but...oh, the feel of his big, solid body against hers was so comforting, so safe.

"Can you get back to your apartment? I need to tell you more but not in public. I've also arranged protection for you. They'll meet you there. Nevertheless, don't go home alone. Is Massimo trustworthy?"

India smiled. "Yes," she said, meeting Massimo's gaze, "I would say Massimo Verdi is trustworthy."

"*Massimo Verdi*? That makes me feel better." Lazlo was relieved. Massimo smiled at her, touching her cheek. India held his hand to her face for a moment, gazing at him.

"Indy, you there? Can you get home?"

India nodded and then realized that was no good to Lazlo.

"Yes, I can get home." She looked at Massimo, who nodded as well. Even if he knew nothing of what was going on, he clearly would be happy to accompany her home. "I'll call you when we get back to my apartment."

She hung up. To give herself a moment, she put her phone away very slowly, taking a deep breath. She looked up to see Massimo watching her, his eyes wary.

"Are you okay, *Bella*?"

India drew in a long breath. "I don't know. Something's happened, and I..." She sighed and tried to smile. "I have to go home. My brother wants to talk to me."

Massimo held out his hand. "I'll walk you back. Listen, you don't have to tell me anything, but I'm here if you need to take a dump on me."

Despite herself, India burst out laughing. "Dude, it's 'dump on me' not 'take a dump on me'. Entirely different, very niche."

He shrugged, grinning good-naturedly.

"My English idioms need improvement."

India smiled at him and stroked her hand down his face. "It's tough to dislike a guy who knows the word 'idioms.' You're perfect." He smirked, deflecting her compliment with a shrug. *He's lovely,* India thought. *Absolutely exquisite.*

She took his hand and they walked through the quiet streets. All the sexual tension had dissipated, and India, despite the horror at Braydon Carter's release, was disappointed. *The timing sucks, that's all,* she thought. Massimo's hand dwarfed hers, his thumb stroking the back of her hand. She moved closer, and he stopped to kiss her again, before walking on. In a few hours, they had forged a connection that wouldn't easily be forgotten.

At her door, Massimo pressed his lips against hers. "I don't think I should impose on you any more tonight, *Bella*. Just promise me, we'll reconnect soon."

India smiled. There was nothing she wanted more than to

invite this gorgeous man into her apartment and make love to him—something that never happened to her—but she couldn't drag him into her mess of a life. "You have my number."

"And you have mine. I'll be disappointed if someone else plays your love interest in your music video."

She laughed. "That won't happen. I'll call you." She hoped beyond hope he didn't realize she was lying.

After he was gone, and she dead bolted her door and checked that her windows were locked, India curled up on the couch and called Lazlo back.

"You okay, bub?" he said.

"Not really. I can't believe they let Carter out, Laz. After everything... *everything*." Her voice broke but she was determined not to cry.

"He won't get near you, Indy, I promise." Lazlo sighed. "The one good thing is that the tour is over, and you can go anywhere. He won't be able to find you."

"Exiled again." India closed her eyes. She knew this all too well: a life of disguise and solitude forced upon her by a man obsessed with her. She had other stalkers—it was an occupational hazard for people in the entertainment business—but no one as relentless, as destructive as Braydon Carter.

No one as *terrifying*.

"How was Massimo Verdi?"

India's heart thumped sadly. "A sweetheart. Surprisingly, a real sweetheart. Damn it."

"I'm sorry, Indy. I wish you would find someone who...well, you know."

India chuckled softly. "I don't need a white knight, Laz. I have you." She sighed. "So, what do you suggest?"

"Leave Venice, obviously. Pick a country and get on a plane.

When you're there, call me, and we'll step up security and find you a place to live. You have your credit cards?"

"Yes."

"Good. Listen, Jess knows about this, too, and she's going to challenge the release."

Jess Olden was India's best friend and her lawyer, a stunningly beautiful woman who was a pit bull in the courtroom. India smiled fondly. "I bet she is. Tell her I love her and thank you."

"I will. Jesus, Indy, I'm so sorry about this. I thought we had finally gotten past this cloak and dagger stuff."

India stared out of the window at the Venetian night and tried not to cry. "Me, too, Laz. Me, too."

Massimo Verdi spent the next few days on a press junket for his new movie but every moment he thought about India Blue: her soft, dark hair that fell below her shoulders, those large brown eyes, and perfect rose lips. He could still smell her delicate scent and his body felt charged and on edge. He needed to see her again; that was now an imperative.

After his last interview, he fended off the meeting requests from his agent and his publicist and retreated to his hotel room, decompressing from talking all day. Massimo enjoyed the junkets to a certain extent, but he also valued his privacy. He changed out of the Saville Row suit he wore and got into a sweater and jeans, flicking on the TV and ordering room service. Before the food arrived, he called Diana, and she grilled him about what happened. "Your note was the opposite of subtle, Diana."

Diana was unrepentant. "So? Did you fuck each other silly?"

Massimo laughed. "No, we didn't. We were interrupted and India had something else to deal with."

"Well, don't let her run away from you, Mass. She has a habit of pulling away even when everyone else can see what she wants. And she wants *you*, believe me. I have never seen her so...befuddled."

"*Befuddled*?" Massimo was curious.

"Okay then, aroused. She was *horny* for you. Can I make it any clearer?" Massimo heard Grey muttering in the background, and Diana clicked her tongue at him. "I'm *not* interfering."

"Do you think it would be inappropriate for me to show up at her door?"

"Go for it. She'll get scared and try to push you away. Don't let her get away, Massi."

After the call, he slowly ate his steak and salad, processing what Diana said. He sensed India might be a flight risk. There was something so vulnerable about her. Why did she look so devastated when her brother called? He grabbed his laptop and did a search on her. *Strange*. For someone so high profile, there was very little information about her on the internet—plenty of gossip and speculation, but actual facts...

Weird.

Massimo closed the laptop and sat back. No, he wouldn't learn a thing from the web about this woman. To get to know her means being with her. He got up and grabbed his coat, stepping out into the cool Venice night. After all, he knew where she lived. He strode through the streets, ignoring the people who stared at him, recognizing their number one movie star.

The doorman at India's apartment building recognized him and let him in with a smile. "How can I help you tonight, Mr. Verdi? Always a pleasure to see you."

Massimo smiled back. "I'm here to see *Signora* Blue, thank you."

"Oh."

Massimo stopped. The doorman looked uncomfortable. "What is it?"

"I'm afraid *Signora* Blue has left, Mr. Verdi."

"Left? You mean she's out for the evening?" Even as he said the words, he knew what the man meant. India had left the building, the apartment, the city.

She was gone.

CHAPTER FOUR - FADED

Helsinki, Finland

India cranked up the heat in the small apartment Lazlo rented for her in the Finnish capital and curled up on the couch to watch the falling snow outside. Everything was covered white in this beautiful city, and it gave India some comfort. Surely, nothing bad could happen in a place like this, right?

Lazlo had this apartment rented for her before she even boarded the plane in Venice; she admired his tenacious, efficient manner. They grew up together, overlooking their fourteen-year age difference, both living with their single mothers in a commune in Canada, living in Maupin's world in San Francisco, and finally settling in a New York apartment with no hot water and only a mattress on the floor. But they were happy. Lazlo's fiery mom, Hanna, was a radical feminist. She and India's mother, the flighty, dreamer Priya, were polar opposites but the best of friends. Even when Lazlo's father had another son, Gabriel, with another woman, and the child was dumped on Hanna to raise, they were a joyous, thoughtful, creative group of nomads, working odd jobs and helping their communities as they had very little themselves.

When Lazlo, Gabe, and India had grown and started earning an income, Hanna refused their help. "I'm happy, my darlings," she would tell them. After India's mom died, Hanna treated India as her own, raising her to be a strong, capable woman, never reliant on a man.

Any man. India sighed. Massimo Verdi wasn't just any man, and yet she ran from him the second she had reason to. Ever since that night, she dreamt of making love to him, that thick cock of his thrusting deep inside her, his full mouth kissing her, thoughts of tangling her fingers in his dark curls.

Those dreamy, green eyes...

Thinking about him wasn't a good idea now that her whole life was on hold again. *God damn you, Braydon Carter! Haven't you done enough?*

The fear of being murdered numbed her; she almost got used to the feeling that her life was limited. Staring out at the snowflakes, she rubbed her abdomen. The scars would always be there; the physical ones faded, but the psychological ones?

Fuck this. India got up from the couch and went to the other room, where a piano stood. She would write songs. That was what she was born to do.

She ran through the tracks she played to Massimo first and began to write a treatment for the video he agreed to costar in. She tore up the first three—all of them way too raunchy for a video—but it improved her mood to daydream about filming sex scenes with Massimo.

Hurting...

As the girl sings the opening bars, she escapes a masquerade ball and runs from her lover after seeing him flirt with another woman. As the pace of the song picks up, a chase through Venice begins as the lover pursues her, desperate to win her back.

As the song reaches the bridge, they face each other across one of the beautiful piazzas. His dark-green eyes are intense, almost dangerous-looking, and she tries to resist but remembers their lovemaking—passionate, uninhibited, a meeting of true soulmates—lovers predestined. As he approaches and takes her in his arms, they dance, almost mirroring their lovemaking. Then masked enemies approach and try to tear the lovers apart. They succeed and the two are buried under a miasma of malevolence. As the song closes, the crowds disperse revealing the man holding his dead lover in his arms as the camera pans out, knowing it was his awful behavior that led to this...

India put her pen down. "Wow, you went dark," she noted. "*Way* dark. *Miasma of malevolence?*" She chuckled and rolled her eyes but there was something about the idea she really treasured. Something...cathartic. She wondered what Massimo would think of it.

For a moment, she chewed on her lip and then grabbed her laptop, doing what she shouldn't do at any cost.

Type the name *Massimo Verdi* into a search engine.

CHAPTER FIVE - PRETTY

January 15th

My darling, my beautiful India,

Every day I wake up and your sweet face is the first I see. I say hello to you before doing anything else and picture you lying next to me. Believing it to be true, I leaned over and pressed my lips against yours.
They taste so sweet, my darling.
As the morning sunshine makes your honey skin glow, we make love, my sexual prowess making you moan and sigh as I fuck you, my cock deep inside your delicious cunt.
In case you're wondering... Yes, I'm pleasuring myself as I write this, pretending it's your hand stroking my prick, playing me the way you play your piano.
All those fans that come to see you, who stand and applaud you, do any of them know what it's like to be inside you? To love you? To taste your blood on their lips?

No. That's my privilege, my sweet darling. Only mine. No one else knows how rich and dark your blood is, how it pumps from you, luscious and hot. I'm the reason you never pose in your underwear like so many other whores in your business. Pity. I'd like to see the scars on your soft belly again, the marks that bind you to me.

And I will, someday, India. I'll see them again, up close and personally.

Soon, my darling, soon.

I love you.

Your Braydon.
 Prisoner 873927555
 ***Texas* State Penitentiary at Huntsville**

CHAPTER SIX - HERE WITH ME

New York City

"Jesus Christ." Lazlo read the letter again as Jess Olden watched his reaction. They were sitting in Lazlo's corporate office on Madison Avenue as Lazlo's eyes grew wide with terror. He put the letter down and rubbed his face. "And this one isn't the worst of them?"

"No. The police are keeping some of the more explicit letters to themselves." Jess sighed. His friend looked tired and stressed. Jess Olden was a beautiful woman, thirty-five years old, her caramel skin from her Chinese mother, her green eyes from her American father. Today there is a pronounced crease between her eyes and dark shadows below. Lazlo studied her. "Jess... did they tell you what was in them?"

Jess hesitated. She was holding back.

"Jess... please. I can't fight this unless I know everything."

"Laz... what they told me was *sickening*. Braydon's obsession with Indy is bizarre. If he finds her, he'll make sure she suffers the torments of the damned before he kills her."

"Fuck." Lazlo buried his head in his hands. "How the hell do they think letting him go will end up? The man is a maniac."

"Yeah, boo. We have to make sure he can't get to her."

"More exile. Indy deserves more. She deserves a *life*."

Jess nodded. "Look, we'll figure it out. The best thing is to try and keep a check on where he is and, God, I don't know, always keep Indy in a different country."

"What kind of life is that?"

"It's *a* life, which is more than Indy gets if Braydon catches up with her."

Lazlo stared out of the window. "She met someone, an actor, the other night. From her voice, I think she liked him. Massimo Verdi."

Jess's eyebrows shot up. "Massimo Verdi? Damn, he's a good-looking man. He's a player."

"That's what I found out." He grinned guiltily at Jess. "I looked him up."

"Big brother."

"Always. But he appears to be a good guy. You say he's a player but that's only in the last few months. He was in a long-term relationship for over a decade. That gives me hope."

Jess laughed. "You got them married off already?"

He chuckled. "Nah, but I heard something in Indy's voice, something I haven't heard in a long time."

"What?"

Lazlo smiled. "Hope."

∼

Los Angeles, California

Massimo Verdi shook the hand of the journalist, concluding his last

Chapter Six - Here with Me

interview of the day. The press junkets for his new film, *Momentum*, were finished, and he could go home now to decompress and relax. Jake, his publicist, smiled at him. "You look relieved."

"You know this is my least favorite part."

They walked out of the hotel suite together. "Your return flight to Rome is in two hours. Danni packed your suitcase already, and the car will pick you up in an hour."

"Thanks, Jake. And thanks for dealing with all this stuff for me." Massimo hesitated. "Any messages?"

Jake ran through the list of calls he fielded for Massimo, but Massimo was disappointed not to hear India's name. *Mio Dio, Verdi, stop thinking about her. She's obviously not interested.*

Except... arrogance aside, he doubted that was true. He felt her quivering when he kissed her, felt her hand cupping his cock. India Blue was an intriguing, enigmatic woman, and he needed more—like a junkie needs another fix.

His attention slid back to Jake when he said, "And Valentina called. She hopes to have lunch when you get back to Rome. She says she did an interview for *Italian Vogue*, and she might have— her words—mentioned a possible reunion."

Jake pulled a face as Massimo groaned. "I'm sorry. All the celebrity rags are running with it."

"Fuck... not your fault, Jake. *Mio Dio,* what's she thinking? The last time we talked..." Massimo blew out his cheeks, forcing himself to calm down. "Never mind, Jake. I'll deal with it. What else?"

"Oh, yeah, I forgot," Jake sorted through some notes. "Here we go. India Blue's people—you know who she is, right? The singer?"

Massimo hid his smile. "Yes, I know who she is." *She occupies my thoughts, day and night.* Jake nodded, not reading the meaning behind Massimo's words.

"Her people got in touch, wanting to know if you'd make an appearance in her next music video."

"Tell them yes," Massimo said without hesitation, and Jake was surprised by his quick reply. Massimo was notorious for keeping people waiting for his commitment to projects. "Tell them yes, whenever, wherever they want me. Whenever *she* wants me."

Understanding crept into Jake's eyes. "Ah," he said with a smile, and chuckled. "Yes, India Blue is..."

Beautiful, sexy, funny. "A great talent."

Jake snorted. "That's the word. *Talented.* And drop-dead gorgeous, which doesn't hurt."

Massimo grinned widely. "Does it ever?"

"You got a crush on her, Mass?"

Massimo laughed. "A little." *A lot.* "Anyway, tell India yes."

"Got it. Oh, and you might want to give the Bellamy's party a miss tonight. Fernanda's going."

Massimo rolled his eyes. "Thanks for that. With her and Valentina..."

Fernanda Rossi was an actress who, like Massimo, was beginning to make strides in the American film scene. She was also a clingy mess, and Massimo counted their one-night stand a few months ago as one of the biggest mistakes in his life. Fernanda was obsessive and jealous; she punched a woman for looking at Massimo at a party. Massimo didn't want drama like that; he didn't want anything to do with Fernanda *ever* again.

Massimo was a rare species in film. Uninterested in the copious amounts of drugs available to stars like him, his biggest vice was sex, especially since the end of his relationship Valentina Acri, a legend in Italian cinema. Valentina, older than Massimo by almost ten years, had guided his career from a young actor into the superstar he was today. He loved her with all his heart, but the children they planned together never came, and by the end of their relationship, they became more like siblings than lovers.

As talented as she was, Valentina, in her late forties, was finding that the roles she craved weren't being offered to her. Her latest interview—the one where she hinted at reconciliation with Massimo—was a ploy to appear younger, vital, still of interest to younger men, cinema's critical target age group between twenty-five and forty-nine. Being with Massimo would achieve that.

Massimo chewed over this and sighed. He owed Valentina his career. How could he not reach out to her? He finished up with Jake and went to his room to get ready to go home. Valentina still kept tabs on where he was at any time, and before now, it didn't bother him much.

Now, for some reason, it irritated him. Valentina knew where *he* was and yet he had no idea where India Blue was. At least her people reached out about the music video; it meant she hadn't written him off completely. Wherever she disappeared to, it must be for a good reason. He wanted to talk to her, though.

In the cab to the airport, he flicked through his phone and typed her name, clicking on the 'News' section. Nothing. Still a ghost. He clicked the *Images* tab and smiled. Jake had seriously underestimated her beauty with the 'drop-dead gorgeous' remark. Her large, deep brown eyes were warm, and her emotions were plain to see within them, even if she herself was guarded. Massimo slotted his ear buds into his ears and found her last album. That *voice*...

He got so lost in her voice that the driver had to call his name twice when they arrived at the airport. Massimo wasn't thinking as he stepped out of the car—and into a melee of press photographers. Los Angeles... He sighed.

"Hey, Massi, you and Valentina gonna get back together?"

Massimo smiled and said nothing as he pushed through to

Check In. His bodyguard, a huge man called Deke, helped him work his way through as flashes went off in his face.

When he was finally installed in his business-class seat, Massimo didn't blame India for her disappearing act; he couldn't imagine she enjoyed this part of fame either.

He idly listened to the pre-flight instructions, snagging his phone to turn it off. It was only then he noticed the text message from an unknown number. He frowned, but a second later, his brow cleared as he read the message, and his heart soared.

Thank you for saying yes. See you soon! Indy x.

CHAPTER SEVEN - RID OF ME

Helsinki, Finland

India played the piano until her fingers ached yet no lyrics would come. She'd been trying to write for days but now, she gave up. No matter, she had enough songs for three new albums. She always pushed herself too hard. She needed to take a break sometimes, but the thought of not writing or playing was anathema to her.

Still, she ran through some cover versions of her favorite songs, throwing a slower version of FKA twigs' "Two Weeks" in there. It made her think of Massimo, with its sensual beat and explicit lyrics. India closed her eyes as she sang, imagining Massimo's hands on her body, his fingertips drifting across her skin, his mouth on hers. Dominating her in bed, his cock plunging inside her over and over, India tangling her fingers in that wild mess of curls on his head, stroking his thick brows, running her fingertips across the long, dark eyelashes... She bit her lip, her body reacting urgently to the thought of him. She grabbed her cell phone. *Fuck this, I want to see him.*

She called Lazlo. When he answered sounding sleepy, she

realized it was still early morning in New York. "Laz, I'm sorry to wake you."

"No matter, Bubba, what's up?"

India took a deep breath. "I'm sick of hiding, Laz. Please, could you call Massimo's people and ask them how soon he could film the video?"

∼

Nashville

After his release from Huntsville, Braydon had been staying at a very nice hotel in downtown Nashville for a month. His benefactor, whose name he still didn't know, arranged a car to pick him up and take him to Nashville. He guessed that flying would leave a paper trail whereas this seemed all very… arranged. He would probably be required to do something for this and he wondered what it would be.

His questions were answered when his benefactor came to see him on the one-month anniversary of his release. He flicked off the television as the man entered the room, flanked by a bodyguard, and Braydon frowned. This dude? Really?

"Hello, Mr. Carter."

Braydon shook his hand, and the other man gestured to a chair. "May I?"

"Go ahead. You're paying for all of this."

The other man sat and gave him a chilly smile. "Yes, I am."

Braydon was struggling to recollect this man's name, but he'd seen him on the news before. By the cut of his suit, he was rich—as if the luxury hotel Braydon was staying in hadn't clued him in. The man's white hair was slicked back neatly, and he wore a signet ring on his left hand with some kind of crest on it. His shoes, Braydon knew, were *Bruno Magli*. He only knew that because he'd just been watching a documentary on O.J. Simpson.

"Well, Mr...?"

The other man smiled. "Just call me... Stanley."

"Well, Stanley, not that I'm not grateful for all of this, but I've been wondering. Why? Why me?"

Stanley nodded. "Fair question and that's why I'm here. You'll be leaving here today, Mr. Carter and travelling to New York City to an apartment that has been purchased for you. There, you will make plans to carry out and complete your mission."

"My mission?" This sounded like a bad movie plot.

Stanley smiled—and Braydon noticed how it didn't travel to the man's eyes. Cold. Ruthless. "Yes, Braydon. I can call you Braydon?"

Braydon nodded. "Sure."

"No need to be concerned, Braydon. From the letters found in your prison cell, apparently you were already planning exactly what I need you to do."

Braydon's eyes widened in shock. "What? You mean...?"

"Yes, Mr. Carter. I want you to kill India Blue."

Rome, Italy

Valentina called him the morning after he returned to Rome, and Massimo arranged to have a lunch with her the following day. His intensely luxurious apartment was situated in the center of the city, and he liked to walk. He was often stopped by fans asking for autographs or selfies and he didn't mind. The day was warm with a light breeze, and he breathed in the fresh air. His decision to appear in India's video was exciting, especially since she had been in contact. He didn't know where she was, but tonight, they were going to see each other face-to-face, albeit over the internet. India was going to video call him to discuss dates and the story for the music video, and he couldn't wait to see her.

Massimo was still smiling when he saw Valentina sitting outside the café, and she raised a hand in greeting. At almost fifty, Valentina was still a spectacular woman: long, wavy, tawny hair, dark blue eyes, and wide smile. She refused to get plastic surgery, so small lines around her eyes and mouth were visible. She chain-smoked, too, and as Massimo kissed her cheek, the scent of cigarettes and perfume was intense. Such a familiar smell; that fragrance meant home to him for many years. Now though, compared to India's scent of fresh linen and clean air, he knew which he preferred.

Valentina turned her head as he went to kiss her other cheek and planted a full kiss on his lips. Massimo pulled back quickly, half-smiling to ease the slight. "Val, you look beautiful."

"Likewise, Mass." She held him at arm's length and studied him as if she were appraising a work of art. "A little more grey, but it suits you."

Massimo smiled. Val was in a flattering mood, which meant she wanted something. They sat and ordered drinks, Massimo looking at the food menu while Val lit another cigarette. "Want one?"

He shrugged and took one, lighting Valentina's for her. "Are you eating today?"

She shrugged and ordered a salad. Massimo, never one to turn down food, ordered *sugo all'arrabbiata* over penne. Val had always looked after her figure, remaining slender and toned. Again, Massimo found himself comparing her sharp edges to India's curves. *Stop it, you're getting obsessed.*

"So, Val... the Vogue interview?"

She had the grace to look sheepish. "I'm sorry, Mass, I did say what they printed. You know why."

"Actually, I don't. You ended our relationship months ago, Val, and you made the right decision. We don't fit anymore." He smiled kindly. "I'll never regret our ten years together. Never. You are my family, Val, but we've moved on. Didn't I see a story about you and Dante Tolani?"

Valentina smiled. "A passing fancy. Dante is sexy, but he's not you, Mass."

Massimo sighed. "Val... listen... There's someone else. Someone I'm... intrigued with."

Valentina gave a brittle laugh. "*Intrigued*? Is that code for fucking?"

"Actually, no. We haven't slept together." *Yet.* But soon, he hoped. An image of India naked and moaning beneath him flashed through his mind, his mouth on hers, then closing around her nipple... His cock was hard against his pants, and he hoped Valentina wouldn't see it and think she was the reason for it.

"Mass, regardless of your newest flame, you're wrong about that. We do fit. I was foolish to throw away our love." She sighed. "No one is better than you, Mass."

That was a change from what she said at the end of their relationship. Massimo would never forget that night; it was seared in his brain.

Immature, irresponsible, and slovenly. Her words to describe him. Those words that caused him the most self-examination. Was he immature? Probably. His days were spent pretending to be another person for money, for Chrissakes. Irresponsible? He still didn't know what that had been about. And slovenly? *Him?* No, he'd take a lot but he wasn't *slovenly*.

Valentine was studying him, reading his mind. "I said a lot of mean things that night, Mass. Too many things. I'm really sorry."

Massimo chewed his lip. "Val... look. We'll always be friends. As for us being together again? No. Too much has passed for that to happen."

For a moment, tears glistened in her eyes, but she rallied. "Can't blame a girl for trying. So, who is she? This new intriguing woman?"

He briefly toyed with the idea of telling her; he was longing to talk to someone about India, but Val wasn't the right person. His potential relationship with India shouldn't be sullied by a bitter ex. And if Val had one failing, it was that she didn't play nice with other women. He couldn't imagine her having the same relationship India had with Diana for instance. He remembered their teasing each other at the dinner table, and he smiled. He wanted more of that fun-loving atmosphere, less of this tension he experienced around Valentina.

They finished lunch and, ever the gentleman, Massimo walked with her to her apartment. She kissed his cheek and met his gaze. "Want to come up?"

Massimo shook his head, smiling again to smooth over the rejection. "No, thanks, Val."

She gave a small, almost incredulous laugh. "You have it bad for this girl. Who is she?"

"Someone I never thought—" he tailed off, not knowing what to say. "Just call it curiosity for now."

Val's expression softened and she touched his cheek. "You used to look like that about me, Massimo. Lucky girl," she whispered and leaned in to kiss him on the mouth.

Neither saw the paparazzo taking pictures of them from across the street. The photographer got a number of shots, then disappeared as Valentina went inside and Massimo Verdi walked away. Two minutes later, he got the call. "Did you get them?"

"I did. My editor's going to love them."

"Good."

Inside her apartment, Valentina smiled to herself and ended the call, dropping her phone onto the table. *Enjoy those pictures, my darling. Your new love won't be happy, and before long you'll come crawling back to me.*

You're mine, Massimo Verdi. Don't ever forget it.

CHAPTER EIGHT - MILLION DOLLAR MAN

Helsinki, Finland

If India was excited to see Massimo again, she tried to rein in the feeling. She'd seen the photographs of him kissing his supposed-ex in the newspapers and on the internet, and she couldn't help the sharp pang of jealousy in her heart.

"Nope. Won't be that girl," she declared and sighed. The universe was telling her, as always, not to get involved; it would only lead to hurt.

India rubbed her head, closing her browser to go take a shower. It was only a few weeks before Christmas and as much as she loved Helsinki, she told Lazlo she wanted to be with him for the holidays, whether it was safe or not.

Lazlo knew she wouldn't be argued with. "Fine. We'll make arrangements to fly you in privately. No arguments about a private plane this time, Indy."

India agreed, but even so, it would be at least another month before she could leave Helsinki. Lazlo agreed on a date in January with Massimo's people to produce the music video, and because of the photos, she was looking forward to it much less.

India dried her long dark hair, then wound it into a bun, dressing in a warm sweater and jeans. Another day at her piano was planned—she had a new album to create, after all—but she felt restless. When her cell phone bleeped with a message from one of her dearest friends, Sun, her spirits lifted immediately.

Sun, his full name Sung-Jae, was a member of one of the hottest K-pop groups on the planet. He and India met at an award show a couple of years ago and clicked immediately. He was five years younger, androgynous, and the most beautiful man India had ever seen. His face had delicate, feminine features, his eyes large and full of expression. His hair was short and neat and frequently dyed to match the project he was working on. His body, however, was as far from feminine as could be possible, with washboard abs, hard pecs and a dancer's body.

They had gone to her hotel room and stayed up all night talking. There was a heat between them they tried to deny, but it had proved impossible, and one night, after another show, they slept together.

Neither wanted a relationship, but their bond was set for life. They never had sex again but often when their paths crossed, they spent the night together, holding each other, talking, and joking around, Sun often teasing Indy about her attempts to learn Korean. He was in love with another member of his group, a quiet, reserved boy called Tae, who was more introverted than the exuberant Sun.

Where are you, Indy? I want to see you!

Her heart ached with warmth. It was easy to adore Sun; he wasn't just beautiful on the outside, but also deep within, too.

I'm away, writing, at the moment. I want to see you, too! Where are you?

Chapter Eight - Million Dollar Man

Back home in Seoul. I can come where you are.

Ha, right! Not without a huge press pack! Have to lay low at the moment. I could go to Seoul.

Come soon. I have a lot to tell you.

Me, too. I'll make the arrangements and get back to you.

Sun sent a smiling emoji along with a heart, and Indy smiled. God, yes, a few days with Sun, and the world would seem a brighter place again. She could tell him about Massimo and ask for his thoughts. He knew about longing for someone.

She could tell Lazlo wasn't happy about her plans. "Indy… those boys get very little privacy. One photo of you and Sun, and Carter might see it."

"Not unless he reads Korean newspapers."

"Don't be naive, India. You know how big that group is. Any whiff of a romance between you and Sun, and it's international news."

India was getting annoyed. "So, now I can't even see my friends? I'm tired of living like this, Laz."

"We're talking about your life, Indy."

"What kind of life is it when I'm trapped, alone, and…" She choked. "What kind of life, Lazlo?" Her voice was a whisper as she fought to stop the tears. "I want to see Sun."

There was a long silence on the end of the phone, and when he spoke again, Lazlo's voice was calmer. "Does this have anything to do with those photographs of Verdi and his ex?"

Fuck, Lazlo knew her so well. "No." *Lie.* "Well, not much. I really do want to see Sun."

"Careful with that boy's heart, Indy." Indy smiled. Lazlo was giving in.

"He's in love with Tae," she said. "I can't break a heart that isn't mine."

Lazlo sighed. "I wouldn't be so sure. There's not much difference in the way he looks at Tae and the way he looks at you. He's just a young man, Indy. Don't confuse him even more."

"I want to see my friend," she insisted, and Lazlo took a deep breath.

"Fine. But we follow the new protocol. Private planes, incognito limos, security at the hotel."

"The environment will hate me with all that jet fuel," she said with regret, but she wanted to be selfish. "Okay, if it means I can see Sun."

"I'll make the arrangements."

Indy thanked her brother and ended the call. Her heart felt lighter, knowing she would see her friend, but still, in the back of her mind, was Massimo. The man was drop-dead gorgeous, lathered in sex appeal and machismo. She could even blame Valentina for not wanting to let him go.

"Listen to yourself, woman," she told herself, "you don't even know this guy or that world."

She sat at the piano and began to play random new melodies, and her mind drifted back and forth between Massimo and Sun, both so different, and yet they were both so desirable in their own ways. She thought about Massimo's kiss, the way his lips commanded hers, the scratch of his stubble. Sun's kiss was soft, his skin was smooth like velvet, his smile sweet and dazzling.

Indy began to smile as a new idea came to mind. Angel and Devil. Sun and Massimo. A concept for her new album. It was just an idea, but it was something to distract herself with. She grabbed her notebook and sat down on the sofa, creating new songs for the rest of the day.

∾

Chapter Eight - Million Dollar Man

New York

Braydon got the call late at night. "She's in Helsinki."

"How do you know?"

His handler laughed. "Carter, we have spies everywhere. The girl is in Helsinki. In the morning, a car will pick you up and take you to the airport. All the details are there. Mr Carter?"

"Yes?"

"Sidney asked me to tell you to make it painful."

Braydon laughed. "I can guarantee that. India will know hell before she dies, I promise."

"Good. I expect to see news of her brutal murder in the newspapers soon."

Braydon dropped his phone and lay back on the bed. At last. Not that it wasn't fun being put up in these luxurious surroundings. The apartment had every mod con and Braydon made the most of it. He cleaned himself up, too, with the expensive clothes in the closet, the ridiculous facial cleansers and moisturizers. A barber came to shave him every day, which Braydon found amusing and slightly irritating.

But he looked a million miles from the scumbag who left prison. He looked almost... respectable. He got up and went to the bathroom, flicking on the light and gazing in the mirror. Would India recognize him now? His face had slimmed down a lot, his hair was greying... but his eyes, that darkness in them burning black, were still the same. He closed them, remembering the day he took her... India was still a kid but breathtakingly beautiful. It entertained him to think that while they were together, it was heavenly for him and hellish for her.

The terror in her eyes, the way she tried so valiantly to fight him off... the shock of the blade sinking into her skin. He was getting an erection from the memory, and he took care of it, grunting and groaning as he jerked off, ejaculating generously.

Shivering and panting hard, he returned to bed, glancing at the clock. It was after midnight. *So it's after 7 a.m. in Helsinki. Is she awake already?* He wished he could telepathically instill fear into her, then snickered at his foolishness. *What is the point if he can't see her terror firsthand?*

Tomorrow would be soon enough. With a forged passport, he can now leave the country. He could hardly wait.

CHAPTER NINE - EVERY BREATH YOU TAKE

Rome, Italy

Massimo was pissed but Valentina was unrepentant. "It's not my fault the paparazzi drew their own conclusions," she stated when he inquired about the photos. "They want us to reunite. What can I do?"

Massimo kept his temper. "Next time, don't kiss me. Let's not risk misunderstandings, shall we?"

Valentina chuckled, a high, tinkly, sarcastic sound. "Well, you could always simply refuse to see me, darling." Her voice dropped to a seductive purr. "But we both know you don't want that."

He ended the call, knowing she had taken the victory. "Fuck!" he yelled into the emptiness of his dwelling. This pissed him off much more this time than ever before... India. They were close to forming a friendship at least, sharing laughs and messages, talking on Skype... Yet, since the photos came out... nada. Zilch!

It felt like a terrible loss to Massimo. He'd be damned if

Valentina's machinations wreck whatever he and India had before it even started.

It wasn't as if he could go see Indy or send her flowers. Where in the world is she? She did not offer information when they spoke last. The only clue he gleaned from their talks was it was somewhere cold because of the sweaters she wore. That could mean anywhere in the Northern Hemisphere—hardly narrowing it down.

Did he dare text her? Would she reply? Fuck it, he has to know.

Hey Bella, hope everything is okay. Looking forward to seeing you in the New Year—although that seems way too long to wait. M.

He made himself put his phone down so he wouldn't check it like some lovesick school kid and left his apartment.

He met his friends for lunch and then strolled around the busy streets of Rome. He was stopped often by fans and admirers, and he gladly signed autographs and took selfies with them. They were the reason he was so popular, after all.

When he got back, he changed clothes before checking his phone, then finally looked at it.

His heart sank. No message.

Fuck. He had seriously blown it?

He called Jake. "Hey, could you call India's people to double-check we're still on for the music video in January?"

"Sure. Any reason?"

"Just haven't heard from her in a while."

Jake caught on. "Ah. The photos."

"Yeah."

Jake sighed. "I'm on it, boss."

Massimo grabbed a pack of cigarettes—he'd been cutting down lately but couldn't quite kick the habit—and went out onto the balcony. The view of the city was spectacular at any time of the day, but at twilight, it took on a sensual, sultry tone that Massimo thought was unequalled.

He remained outside, staring over the city until it grew dark and he tired. He walked into the apartment and saw a message on his phone.

Hey, of course. Looking forward to working with you. India.

Even if it lacked the warmth they had built up, this was something. But he had definitely lost ground. If he wanted to pursue India the way he hoped, he needed to avoid debacles with Valentina or any other woman.

He was in too deep now; he had to follow through. India Blue was too special of a woman to let go of that easily; he felt it in his bones.

He read her message a few more times, then, almost satisfied, went to bed.

~

Helsinki, Finland

India was half-pleased, half-annoyed by the message from Massimo. *I see you, Verdi. I know guilt.* But she couldn't deny it pleased her.

Early morning, she'll be flying to Seoul. She could hardly wait. She needed her buddy, her confidante, and damn it, she needed his arms around her. Nothing brought her peace like being in Sun's sweet presence.

She wanted to find a gift for him, something Finnish and fun. She pulled on her heavy sweater and coat, then donned a wool hat snugged down over her hair, stuffing her long, thick strands under it. She completed the look with no makeup and thick, black-framed spectacles. No one could recognize her like this.

She walked into the city center, through crowds of early Christmas shoppers and lost herself in the shops. She forgot what it was like to be free to do this—but then again, she wasn't exactly alone. The security team that followed her here kept a respectful distance, but she knew they were there. Out of the corner of her eye, she would suddenly spot one of them and want to play games with them—losing herself in a throng of shoppers so they'd panic, only to appear behind them, touching them on the shoulder as she passed to let them know she was kidding.

On lock-down, you found your games where you could. India located a small gift shop that sold knickknacks and oddities she knew Sun would love. His quirky personality, plus his youth, meant his bedroom was stuffed with things like this, models of superheroes and anime characters. Sometimes India felt more like his big sister than his sometime-lover, and she wondered if they had already settled into those roles. It had been a couple of years since they last saw each other, after all.

Afterward, she wanted to have some hot chocolate in a cafe. Someone moved beside her. "Ms. Blue... perhaps we've been out too long?"

It was one of her security guards, Nate. She smiled. "Let me have some hot chocolate and we can go."

He nodded. "Top floor. There's an elevator."

Only two other people were in the elevator: a middle-aged woman and a man with bright bleach-blonde hair and too-blue eyes behind thick-rimmed glasses. India nodded politely, then looked away. Nate silently rode with her but kept his distance as they arrived at the café.

India ordered a cup of hot chocolate and sat at a table near the window, looking down over the streets. The evening was settling in and later, as she walked back to her residence, she realized she'd miss this place. She planned on staying in Seoul until she goes home for Christmas, but she enjoyed her time in this country and this city.

She knew Nate and the other bodyguard were close, but suddenly she stopped, her skin prickling as her sixth sense kicked in.

Someone is watching me.

She scanned the streets but it was a crapshoot.

Recognize *him*.

She turned, shot a look at Nate, who sensed that something was wrong. He made his way closer as someone from behind bumped into her.

"Sorry," the person muttered, walking past, then turning to look at her.

It was the guy from the elevator. Extremely blue eyes. *Contact lenses*, she realized. Fear was clutching at her chest but then Nate was beside her, taking her by the arm and gently steering her.

He didn't leave her side until she was in the apartment. He sat her down. "What was it?"

India blew out her cheeks. "You'll think I'm insane, but I got the craziest feeling that someone was watching me. Not you or Tom. Someone bumped into me... he was the guy from the elevator."

"The blonde guy?"

She nodded.

"Did he touch you?"

India shook her head. "Only bumped my shoulder. It's probably nothing, coincidence."

Nate didn't look happy. "Damn it."

"Nate, it's probably a mishap and just me being paranoid." She felt foolish and careless. She shouldn't put Nate and Tom in such situations. Sure, it was their job but...

"I'm sorry, Nate. I shouldn't have gone out."

Nate shook his head. "You can't completely hide away, Indy, and it was low-risk. Don't worry about it. I'll check in with Tom. You're okay?"

"Of course. Thank you, Nate."

"Anytime."

Indy took her coat off, only now noticing there was a tear in the back of it. She frowned. How did that happen? She shrugged. Did it matter?

She walked into her bedroom, peeling off the sweater that was getting hot and itchy. Tugging it over her head, she threw it on the bed and went to the bathroom, cranking on the shower and stripping the rest of her clothes off.

She sighed with relief as the hot water streamed down her body, and she took her time, shaving and buffing, then stepped out and massaged body lotion into every inch of her skin. India never felt sexier than when she was freshly showered, and she felt a thrill of excitement go through her when she thought of seeing Sun tomorrow. She toyed with a brief fantasy of being made love to by him and Massimo Verdi at the same time, both men such polar opposites, but what a turn on...

She was still smirking when she returned to her bedroom and put on the cotton nightshirt. She picked up the sweater to put it in her half-packed suitcase—and froze. An envelope lay on the bed. Her name was handwritten across it in a scrawl she recognized.

Instantly she knew.

"Nate!"

She didn't mean to scream in such a panic, but Nate came rushing in, followed by Tom.

India pointed to the envelope. "Did either of you put this here?"

They shook their heads. Indy's knees gave way, and Tom

caught her as Nate grabbed the envelope and ripped it open. Her bodyguard's face paled.

"Is it from him?" She asked, her voice barely a whisper.

Nate, his expression one of shock, nodded. "Yes. It's from Carter."

He found her.

CHAPTER TEN - PERFECTLY LONELY

My darling, India,

Surprise! Did you really think you could hide from me? Didn't my letters suggest what your future would be?
I'll always be with you, beautiful girl, until the moment you take your last breath.
It won't be long now.
Yours, always,

Braydon.

India sat on the plane, her ruined coat over the nightshirt, jeans hastily pulled on. Nate barely gave her time to throw the rest of her belongings into a case before he and Tom spirited her away. They took a long and complicated route to the airport, making sure they weren't being followed. Only when Nate was satisfied, they made their way to the runway and the small private jet that idled there.

Now India was alone in the cabin, wondering how the hell Carter found her, of all places, in Helsinki. She was so careful when speaking to her friends, her colleagues—only Lazlo knew she was in Helsinki.

Lazlo... and Gabe. Her other pseudo-brother, Lazlo's half-brother, but she couldn't imagine Gabe would tell her would-be murderer where she was. No freaking way, she told herself again, ignoring the nagging doubt.

Gabe would never hurt her... but he was also a drunk with a big mouth, having always lived in Lazlo's imposing shadow. Gabe was the playboy of the family, never being faithful to a single girlfriend, not even the last one, Serena, whom Lazlo and India adored. Indy recalled the day Gabe admitted to cheating on her. Indy yelled, he yelled back, and their relationship had never been the same since. Serena thanked India for taking her side and promised to stay in touch but she drifted away. It was because she didn't want to get between Indy and Gabe's friendship.

Indy was still ticked about it, and Gabe distanced himself, but she couldn't imagine he would sell her out to the man who wants to kill her.

... the moment you take your last breath...

Jesus. She insisted on reading the letter, and when she called Lazlo, she told him point-blank. "Show me the letters! I want to see them," she requested when Lazlo admitted he had them.

"No. No way."

"Laz... there's protecting me and then there's treating me like a child. Do you think I will be shocked? After what he did to me? I want to see them."

She must have hit a nerve with Lazlo because a few minutes after she hung up, Jess called her. Lazlo always got Jess to call her on professional matters when she was in trouble.

Jess and Indy went back years, their friendship cemented in college. There was a point when Indy thought she might be in love with Jess, who was bisexual, but the crush faded into sisterhood. Unlike Lazlo, Jess was the person who could stand up to Indy when she was on a tear. The first word out of Jess's mouth was "No! No way, dude. You're not seeing these pieces of filth."

"Dude," which was how they referred to each other. "Come on. Are they really worse than getting stabbed and left for dead?"

"India... they will haunt you forever if you read them. They are not about *me,* and they give me sleepless nights! The thought of you reading them, knowing what he wants to do to you... *No!*"

That made India feel bad. "You're not sleeping?"

"Take the worst thing that could happen to someone you love and multiply it by a thousand. Would *you* be able to sleep?"

"Oh, Jess."

Jess was clearly upset, and India heard her ragged breathing. "Okay... all right, Jess. I... if I knew what to expect..."

"What he did to you before... compared to what he's planning? That's nothing. He's not talking murder, Indy, he's talking slaughter."

India was speechless. She closed her eyes and took a deep breath. For a moment, neither said a word. Then Jess cleared her throat. "You're going to visit Sun?"

"Yes. I can't wait to see him, actually."

"He's an angel. If anyone can take your mind off this, it's him." Jess adored Sun; she treated him like her little brother, and the feeling was mutual. Sun found Jess's no-bullshit approach to everything entertaining. "And I heard about some Italian movie star. What's happening there?"

"Complications." India sighed. "But I keep thinking about him."

"Did you fuck yet?"

India chuckled. "No, Laz ran a good cockblock on that with news about Carter. But I would have."

She giggled, her friend making her feel less tense. "Do you *want* to fuck him?"

"Yes." Indy answered before she could lie about it. "I would fuck that man for hours. I might regret it, but I would."

Jess laughed. "That's my girl."

"If you promise not to tell anyone... I have a fantasy about having both Sun and Massimo at the same time."

Jess whooped. "Now that really *is* my girl!"

India laughed, although her face was burning. "It's not something I've ever done."

"Really? Well, welcome to the jungle, dude."

"You have?"

"Two men at the same time? Many times." Jess gave a throaty, dirty snicker. "Girl, if the opportunity presents itself, go for it."

India sighed. "Only we could go from discussing bloody murder to threesomes and orgies."

"Oh, sweets. Well, that's what we do. Your safety comes first! If it helps to joke about it, I'm all for that. Love you, dude."

"Love you too, Slutty Dude."

"You know it."

India's tense shoulders had eased as she chatted with Jess, and when the call ended, she went to the bedroom at the rear of the plane. The jet was Lazlo's baby, and even though India nagged him about his carbon footprint, she was glad that he had it now. Her destination can be kept more private by going to three different airports before heading to South Korea.

She took an Ambien, and it wasn't until after they landed and taken off again from Charles de Gaulle in Paris that she woke. She took a shower and went to find food. Some hot food was bought for her in Paris, and she indulged gratefully, asking Nate and Tom if they'd eaten.

"We have, thanks," Nate retorted. "Listen, do you mind if I sit for a time and talk with you?"

Indy smiled at him. "No problem, as long as you don't mind watching me eat this steak like a starving puma."

"Ha, not at all."

India began to eat as Nate sat down. "What's up?"

"I'd like to go over how we're upping the security in Seoul. I know," Nate held his hands up as Indy grimaced, "but this affects Sun and his group as well, so we had to coordinate something."

"Of course," Indy felt ashamed. "No one is going to hurt Sun. I'd stand in front of a bullet for him."

"Well, let's hope the precautions we've taken means *no one* gets hurt. We still don't know how Carter found you in Finland."

Indy looked away from Nate's stare. He was probably thinking *it's Gabe.* Gabe and his drinking and bragging about his famous 'sister.' "Okay, so what's the plan?"

"Sun's apartment building is staked out by press night and day, so you can't go there. We and his security team have worked out an arrangement. There's an apartment on the outskirts of the city. It's rented in a false name, has no cameras, and is very quiet. Sun's being taken there now. You'll join him when we land."

"Christ," Indy exclaimed. "He's really being inconvenienced. What about his management, the rest of his group?"

"Your timing is great. They're taking a break for the remainder of the year. They just finished a world tour. Management wants them to rest."

"It's about time. Have you seen their schedule? It's insane."

Nate smiled at her. "Sun sent a message. We replied that we had to change your number because of the security breach. He said to tell you he can't wait to see you."

Indy felt a rush of warmth. Seeing Sun would be like a shot

of pure joy. She chewed on her steak for a moment. "The new number... who has it?"

"Security, Lazlo, Jess, the usual. Not Gabe," he added. and they exchanged a look.

"Good. It's not like we're talking at the moment anyway."

"One of the avenues we're looking at is that someone got your private number and traced it. Someone with money."

"Obviously. Carter wouldn't have that kind of money, would he?"

Nate shrugged lamely. He knew something he wasn't comfortable sharing. He can keep his secrets for now. "Nate?"

"Yes?"

Indy put her fork aside. "Massimo Verdi. Does he have the new number?"

"Do you want him to have it, Indy? Do you know him well enough to trust him?"

India wanted to say yes so badly, and the thought she might not speak or text with Massimo until after the New Year hurt... but did she trust him?

No.

She couldn't get those photographs out of her mind even though she had no right to be jealous—especially as as she was about to spend time with another man.

"No," she said, finally. "Let's not drag him into this. He can do it through Lazlo."

"I agree. The fewer people have your new number, the better. Anyway, we might have to use burner phones from now on or at least until they get Carter."

India sighed. "Get him? He's out of prison, Nate. As far as they're concerned, he hasn't committed a crime, so how exactly will they *get* him?"

"The letters are enough reason to bring him back. They're death threats, Indy. When they catch him, he's going away. He won't get near you again, I promise." He smiled. "Changing the subject, someone else wants to talk to you."

"Who?"

"Your father."

India rolled her eyes. " *No*, thanks."

"Are you sure?"

"Entirely. I have nothing to say to him."

Nate studied her. "He's a powerful man; he might be able to help."

"But he won't." India's hard tone made it clear they were done talking about her estranged father. "Look, let's discuss how it'll work when we get to Seoul."

Rome

Massimo tried her number again only to receive a dead tone. Wow. She must be really pissed at him.

Fuck it. I blew it.

Or rather Valentina had. She was a master manipulator. He was so angry at her, he could scream!

Massimo tried India's number one last time, then dialed Diana's number in England.

"Hello, handsome."

"Hey, Diana... how are you?"

"You mean how is *India* after she saw the photos of you and your ex?"

Diana knew him so well, and he couldn't help but chuckle. "Valentina's work."

"I thought as much but that won't help convince India you're worth a shot. She's extremely skittish."

"What's with her? The night we met, a call from her brother spooked her pretty bad."

There was hesitation in Diana's voice. "It's really not my place to tell you. I could say look her up on the internet, but they've managed to scrub everything relating to... Look, something happened when she was younger and it left a scar. Physically and mentally."

That made him more curious. "Something happened? Someone hurt her?"

"I've said more than enough already, Massi. Look... give her some time. If you really like her, if it's meant to be—and in my heart, I know it is—it will happen. But move on with your life until then. That's the best advice for you."

He met some friends for drinks later, but he found himself preoccupied by what Diana said. Someone hurt India? More than likely it was something very serious; the fact that it was scrubbed off the internet was pretty weird. Didn't people usually exploit their pain in this industry?

Jesus. His mind was rampant with theories on what happened. Even more insidious was the sense they missed their chance, that the incredible heat of their first meeting had long since dissipated, and by the time they met again in the New Year, it would have totally vanished.

Fuck.

He was getting too hung up on a woman who was possibly lost. *Screw it.* Later, he and his friend Ricardo went to a club, and when a sensational redhead made eyes at Massimo, he pushed all thoughts of India Blue aside and took the redhead to his apartment.

The redhead—whose name he couldn't remember—was a great fuck, and she distracted Massimo for a few hours. By the time she let herself out at dawn, he was sated, exhausted, and grateful she knew the rules of the game—after all, it was just sex. He slept for a few hours but then woke to the news that Valentina was involved in a serious car crash.

He was on the way to the hospital before the anchor finished reporting the headline.

CHAPTER ELEVEN - ANGEL

Seoul, South Korea

"I swear, Sun, you get more beautiful every time I see you."

He grinned at her, the highpoints in his cheekbones coloring. As celebrated as he was, Sun was shy and humble about his beauty. "I could say the same, Indy."

He wrapped his arms around her and held her tightly. India sank into his embrace. He'd grown: he stood five-ten and was much manlier. Being held by him was bliss. He tenderly kissed her forehead and smiled.

"I missed you, Sunbeam."

They were in the rented residence, India having arrived only a few moments ago. The feeling of relief and joy at seeing her friend was overwhelming, and tears were welling up in her eyes.

"Oh... don't cry, Indy! Let's sit down and catch up!"

They lay down and cuddled on the vast couch, Sun pulling a fluffy yellow blanket around them. They always did this, swaddled together while they talk. It felt safe and a million miles away from the rest of the world.

"I'm sorry you had to upend your life because of me, Sun. You'll never know how grateful I am."

He shook his head. "Don't be. It actually worked out... Tae... Tae and I needed some time apart."

"You and Tae are together?" He shook his head.

"Not as such... we can't be together like that. It would be a scandal here... but it's hard to deny the attraction, especially after Tae said he feels it, too."

"That's wonderful!"

Sun shook his head. "No. It makes it worse. The longing."

"Oh, Sun..."

He buried his face in her neck and sighed as she held him tighter. "He loves you," she whispered.

"And I love him. It's agony."

It was sad to see the tears on his sweet face. She gently wiped them away. "Don't cry, beautiful boy."

"I'm glad you're here, Indy. I need you."

"Right back at you, baby."

He kissed her then, softly on the mouth. "Why is love so complicated? How can I be in love with two people at the same time?"

India smiled at him. "What we have is... we're soulmates, Sun, you and I. We transcend sex. You'll always be my guy, whether you're with Tae forever—I know that's your future—or perhaps...I meet someone."

Sun studied her face. "You *did* meet someone."

"Maybe. I don't know." She never lied to Sun, ever. She couldn't do something so cruel to such a pure heart. She told him about Massimo. "I just don't know, Sun. He's not what I need. He's a player and a freaking movie star. Someone who may still be hung-up on his ex."

"How long were they together?"

"Ten years, I think."

Sun grimaced. "Ouch."

"See?"

Sun propped himself on his elbow. "What was the chemistry like?"

"Insane. Like you and me when we first met."

"Wowser."

She grinned. "Wowser?" Sun's English was exemplary, but she was always surprised when he came up with idioms and slang.

Sun stroked his finger down her cheek. "You like him."

Indy nodded. "But I don't know if he's healthy for me."

"Not everything has to be long-term. Fuck him if that's what you want."

Indy snuggled to him. His skin was so soft she could hardly believe it. "For now, selfishly, I just want to be with you."

Sun pulled her closer. "Then you have me, Indy."

Later, she and Sun made dinner, a soft tofu stew with plenty of sticky rice and vegetables, and homemade kimchi that made India's mouth water. They ate, talking and laughing over the silliest of things.

After dinner, they lounged on the couch playing computer games and watching funny videos online until Indy was tired.

Sun pulled her up off the coach, and they walked hand-in-hand to the bedroom. There never was any doubt they would share a bed; they always had.

Sun undressed her, chuckling as she could barely keep her eyes open, and he steered her onto the bed, pulling the blanket over her. Indy stirred when he slipped in naked beside her. Sun kissed her forehead. "Good night."

Indy tried to protest, but then Sun was cradling her in his

arms and singing softly to her, and she, unable to resist the peace it brought her, sank into a deep slumber.

The light in the room was blue when she woke shivering, from a horrific nightmare where blood and terror mingled with love, hurt, and heartbreak. India panted for air, her jaw stiff from clenching. She looked at Sun, his otherworldly beauty even more pronounced in the moonlight.

India lay back down and gazed at him. Sun was her safe place, she realized. He opened his eyes and smiled at her. They lay in silence for a moment, then Sun moved closer and kissed her.

It seemed natural to have him move on top of her, his angelic face such a contrast to his well-toned body. His hands smoothed down her skin, caressing her with the lightest touch and yet every place they brushed felt like it was set aflame. India gazed at him. "Sun?"

Was he sure that his love for Tae wouldn't be sullied if they made love tonight?

"This is our bubble," Sun whispered, "And I love you."

"I love you too, Sunbeam."

It was a special kind of love; it wasn't something that could ever be tangible, but right now, it was what they needed. Sun kissed her again, this time with more urgency, and India responded, losing herself in his soft eyes and incredible body.

By the time he was inside her, India's body had taken over completely, and at first, they moved slowly together, but soon took on an intensity that she needed.

After she came, India did something she hardly ever did. She cried! Sun wrapped her in his arms and held her until she was cried out. Then he kissed her and said he loved her once more.

They fell asleep as the sun rose, and India knew she made the right decision to come here.

She just prayed that whoever was funding Brayden Carter wouldn't trace her. She needed some time. She needed time and for Sun to not be in danger. She needed time.

And she needed peace.

CHAPTER TWELVE - LOVE IS A LOSING GAME

Rome, Italy

Massimo smirked when he saw the apparent relief on the hospital staff's faces as Valentina was discharged. Three days and she had made their lives hell with her demands and histrionics. The 'serious' injuries were nothing more than whiplash and a sprained wrist but Valentina insisted on several unnecessary tests. "What if there's something wrong with my brain? What if I can't drive again?"

The kicker was she wasn't driving the vehicle that had crashed anyway. The doctor could not help rolling his eyes, stopping when he saw Massimo watching, but Massimo winked at him. He understood.

Now, Massimo sighed as he wheeled Valentina out to a hoard of paparazzi—notified by her, of course—and he wanly smiled through their barrage of questions. Valentina, bedecked in an 'Audrey Hepburn' sunglasses-and-scarf get up, waved imperiously and gave her thanks to the staff. She managed to put her hand on Massimo possessively the whole way through but this time Massimo didn't care. When a paparazzo asked him if the two were together, he looked at the man's camera directly and shook his head. "No. We're just good friends."

Valentina waited until they were in the car before she took her sunglasses off and when she did, Massimo could see her rage. "Why did you say that? Why?"

"Because it's the truth, Val. We are not a couple. You were the one to end it, and now I'm telling you it's over. You will not manipulate me again."

"Yet you were the first to come to the hospital." Valentina took out one of her cigarettes and lit it, offering him the slim silver case—always affectionate in everything she did. Massimo shook his head as she snapped the case shut in irritation. "Is this about your singer?"

Massimo stiffened. "How do you know about India?"

Valentina smiled victoriously. "I have my sources. And she's disappeared off the map. Must be frustrating for you."

"India is none of your business."

Valentina's expression went cold. "Stop pretending to be something you're not, Massimo. You're a whore and apparently that woman doesn't play games. She'll see right through you."

She already has. "Maybe I've changed." He realized it was a mistake as soon as the words came out of his mouth. Valentina laughed.

"*Sure* you have, darling. And that redhead coming out of your apartment the day I had my accident, who was she? Your French tutor?"

Massimo grit his teeth. "I'm not pretending to be a saint, Val, either in my past or now. If and when I see India again, I'll do what it takes for her to trust me."

"You're fooling yourself." Valentina waved a dismissive hand, and Massimo turned to stare out of the window.

Maybe I am kidding myself, he thought, *but fuck it, I want to try*. He had a plan in place already. In three days, he will go to New York and talk to India's brother, Lazlo. Using the cover of discussing the music video, he will try and make friends with the man, to prove he could be trusted. Find out what happened to make her so elusive. It was worth a shot.

She was worth a shot.

∼

New York City

Braydon listened to his yelling liaison for a good ten minutes before he got a word in. "You *had* her. She was there. You could have finished the job. India Blue should be dead, you asshole, *dead!* It should be all over the news, her fans should be holding mass vigils, memorial concerts thrown by her music colleagues. Instead she's in the wind... *again!*"

Braydon had enough. "Listen, you little weasel, I don't answer to you. Your boss knows I will kill her but she has body guards. It was by chance I got that close. I don't want it to be half-assed. She survived the last time. You have no idea what I did to her. So, fuck you, *asshole*. I told you I'd do it and I will."

By the end of his rant, he was listening to a dead tone and in a rage, he threw his cell phone at the wall where it smashed into a million fragments. *Screw it.* Stanley's money could buy him a new one.

Calming himself, he sat down and made notes. India was gone, spirited away. Leaving the note in her apartment had been a dumb move, but the temptation to scare her proved too much to resist.

So, what now? He thought about the ways he could find out where she was and really, the easiest way was to get to her brothers. He knew the younger brother, Gabriel, was a drunk; he learned that when he asked how they found her in Helsinki.

"The brother's a drunk and big mouth. He likes to talk about his famous sister. It didn't take us long to feed him enough booze and cocaine and set him up with a hooker. He gave up the information easy enough."

Indeed, Gabe Schuler was an option. Although Carter found her in Helsinki, they figured out Gabe was the weak link. He would bet the farm that Gabe didn't know where she was now.

Which left him with the older brother, and Carter didn't like the idea of taking on Lazlo Schuler. Schuler had a reputation as a nice guy—until he was crossed or until his family was threatened. Braydon followed India's career while he was in prison and knew Lazlo managed everything. He had assistants, of course, and Braydon concentrated on finding out who else ran India's career. She was famous for being extremely private and not taking publicity away from her records or concerts, so she had hired others to handle that.

The first name he came up with was a woman in Los Angeles: Coco Conrad was a publicist, a very successful one, who handled everything for India on the west coast. He would start there. He booked a ticket for the next day.

In his bathroom, he stripped off, stepping into the shower. He needed to look different from the Viking he was in Finland. There was no recognition in India's eyes after he bumped into her, neither did she noticed when he slashed her coat with a razorblade. It was a half-hearted swipe; he didn't actually want to hurt her in case she screamed and alerted those damn bodyguards.

It would all be over if they'd caught him then. He'd never get another chance. Even the scent of her perfume drove him mad. He passed her, turning to look back... In the flesh, she was more beautiful than he remembered: those huge brown eyes, her sweet face, that perfect mouth.

He had tasted those lips and knew their softness. Knew the shape of them when she screamed bloody murder. He couldn't wait to see that again.

Concentrate. He dyed the bleached hair black, exasperated when it turned a dirty, almost green color. He tried again and this time it seemed to stick. He inserted dark brown contact lenses and applied the fake beard. *Yes. This is good.* Thankfully he wouldn't need another fake passport inside the country, but Stanley's people provided him with enough different photo IDs with disguises to travel with ease within the States.

Braydon tried to figure out his approach to Coco Conrad. He could act as a newbie film producer looking for representation. She wouldn't take him on, of course, not when she can pick and choose her clientele but he might be able to charm her. If she would accept his dinner invitation…

Finally done with his disguise and happy with it, he removed the fake beard, laying it on the bathroom counter to wear it in the morning and switched the light off. It was after midnight. He checked his email alerts; no news about India Blue.

Braydon went to bed, thinking about her lips again. *Not long now*, he told himself as he finally went to sleep.

New York City

Lazlo Schuler worked past midnight, catching up on other clients, then sat back and sighed, exhausted with work and strain. India was hidden away in South Korea with Sun, and he hoped she was finding peace. Lazlo felt constantly on edge and paranoid, but he couldn't imagine what it must be like to live under a death threat, to never be able to put down roots, to never having relationships.

He hoped India and Sun cared for one another. He respected Sun; Lazlo was a man who was comfortable in his heterosexuality, but even *he* would turn for Sun—the guy was stunning. More than that, Sun was exactly who India needed right now: kind and funny with a big heart.

Lazlo examined the message his PA brought in. Massimo Verdi. He wanted to meet in a couple of days and it probably wasn't representation he wanted to talk about.

Lazlo had doubts about the man. The photos with his ex, the rushing to her side after the accident, and his denials they were together afterward. Verdi's playboy life is shining through. Regardless of whether he and India shared an attraction, Massimo Verdi was trouble. Lazlo could see India's disappointment after the photos of Massimo and his ex were published, and he knew she would let that go.

Besides, he sighed, India didn't need much reason to run away—not that he blamed her, but he hoped she wasn't using Sun. He deserved better, and India would be horrified at the thought of that.

He tried to call her but got no answer. It was rather early in Seoul so he wasn't alarmed. He heard someone walking into the office and frowned.

"Laz?"

Shit. Gabe. At least he sounded sober. That was a rarity. "Gabe, in here."

His half-brother smiled as he came into the office. "Hey, bro." Gabe was wary, the result of being chewed out by Lazlo after the Helsinki debacle.

Lazlo nodded. "Hey. It's late."

"Look, it's been bugging me, but I want to say again how

Chapter Twelve - Love is a Losing Game

sorry I am. I'd never knowingly put Indy in danger, you know that. I hope she knows it, too."

Lazlo scrutinized his brother. "Giving up the booze and nose candy would go a long way towards that."

"I was thinking of calling her."

Lazlo shook his head. "No. Sorry, Gabe, that won't happen. We can't trust you."

Gabe sighed. "Yeah. I don't trust myself these days."

"What is it, Gabe? What's driving you lately? First the stuff with Serena and now this? Plus... how much coke do you snort? You're always so wired."

Gabe rubbed his face. "You're right, okay? But I'm stuck in this loop where if I don't snort, then I'm exhausted, like, dead to my bones."

Lazlo leaned forward. "Go to a rehab. I'll pay for that."

"I can't take more money from you, Laz."

"You can if it'll turn your life around. When you're sober, you can work for me. The city isn't good for you."

Gabe nodded, staring out of the window at the city. "Fine. But then I pay you back."

Lazlo sighed, relieved. Gabe was a problem he didn't need at the moment. "Good."

There was a long silence. "Does she hate me?" Gabe's voice quivered, but he coughed to cover his nervousness. Lazlo softened.

"Of course she doesn't, Gabe. *Of course* not. She might be angry for a while, but she loves you like you love her. She was pissed about Serena but then, so were all of us. You fucked up the best thing that ever happened to you."

"I know." Gabe sat back in his chair. "I've been trying to call her but she won't talk to me, not that I blame her. Jeez." He smiled sheepishly. "It would probably help if I stopped catting around."

Lazlo snorted. "Perhaps. Who's the latest."

"Italian actress called Fernanda Rossi. Seriously hot redhead, incredible in bed."

That name ring a bell. "Didn't she fuck Massimo Verdi a few months back?"

Gabe rolled his eyes. "Yup. She never stops talking about how he dumped her without a second glance. Fucker."

"Glass houses, Gabe."

Gabe chuckled. "Touché." He got up. "Look, I'll find a place to get help and let you know, okay? I'll find meetings, too. AA and NA. This is a wake-up call, I mean it. If anything happened to Indy because of me... I couldn't live with it." He chewed his lip. "Are you in touch with her?"

Lazlo nodded and Gabe sighed. "Tell'er I love her, would you? Tell her I'm sorry and I miss her. Tell her I'll do anything to make things good with her and hope she finds justice with this asshole. Laz, if I'd ever catch up with Carter, I'll kill that son of a bitch myself."

"On that, brother, we can agree."

After Gabe left, Lazlo drove home. His work took all of his time, and although India was always at him to carve time out for solitude, the truth was Lazlo loved his work. He had random hook-ups but nothing permanent, and he couldn't be bothered unless he really liked someone, and that hasn't happened since...

Best not think about *her*. It was too painful. Not even Indy knew about the woman he loved and lost. That drove him to work harder and to protect his sister. He knew what fanatical love could do.

Not that he thought what Carter felt for India was love. The guy was a psychopath, pure and simple.

You won't get what you want, Carter, not this time. You will not put one finger on my little sister if it takes me killing you myself.

This time, Carter, the only one who will be dead is you.

If you want to continue reading this story,
you can get your copy from your favorite
vendor by searching for the title:

His Hidden Love
A Reverse Harem Romance Their Secret Desire Book 1

You can also find the e-book version by
typing this link in your computer's
browser:

https://www.hotandsteamyromance.com/products/his-hidden-love-a-holiday-romance-their-secret-desire-book-1

OTHER BOOKS BY THIS AUTHOR

Saving Her Rescuer: A Billionaire & A Virgin Romance

I was just trying to get away from my crazy ex for the weekend when I ended up in a giant pileup on the highway up to Gore Mountain.

https://geni.us/SavingHerRescuer

∽

Sensual Sounds: A Rockstar Ménage

Lust. Lies. Double lives.

The rock and roll industry is full of people who are looking out for themselves and willing to do anything to rise to the top.

https://www.hotandsteamyromance.com/collections/frontpage/products/sensual-sounds-a-rockstar-menage

∽

On the Run: A Secret Baby Romance

Murder. Lies. Fraud. Just another day in the lives of billionaires and women on the run.

https://www.hotandsteamyromance.com/collections/frontpage/products/on-the-run-a-secret-baby-romance

∽

The Dirty Doctor's Touch: A Billionaire Doctor Romance

I am a master. An elitist. I am at the top of my field, and I know what I am doing.

https://www.hotandsteamyromance.com/collections/frontpage/products/the-dirty-doctor-s-touch-a-billionaire-doctor-romance

∽

The Hero She Needs: A Single Daddy Next Door Romance

He's the only man I've ever wanted...

https://www.hotandsteamyromance.com/collections/frontpage/products/the-hero-she-needs-a-single-daddy-next-door-romance

∽

You can find all of my books here:

Hot and Steamy Romance

https://www.hotandsteamyromance.com

∽

Facebook

facebook.com/HotAndSteamyRomance

©Copyright 2020 by Alizeh Valentine – All Rights Reserved
In no way is it legal to reproduce, duplicate, or transmit any part of this document in either electronic means or in printed format. Recording of this publication is strictly prohibited and any storage of this document is not allowed unless with written permission from the publisher. All rights are reserved.
Respective authors own all copyrights not held by the publisher.

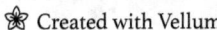 Created with Vellum

www.ingramcontent.com/pod-product-compliance
Lightning Source LLC
LaVergne TN
LVHW021716060526
838200LV00050B/2695